CHAPTER ONE

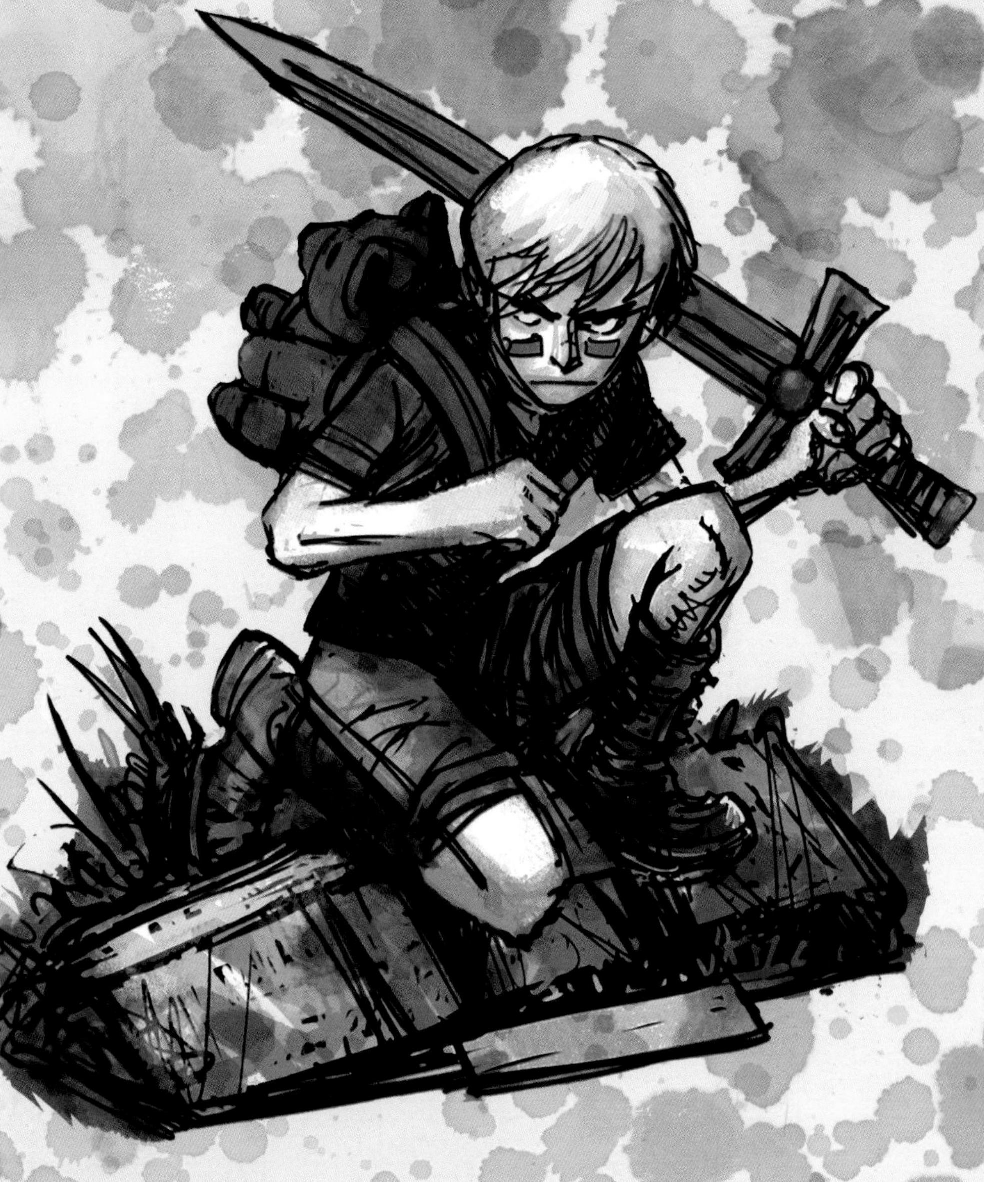

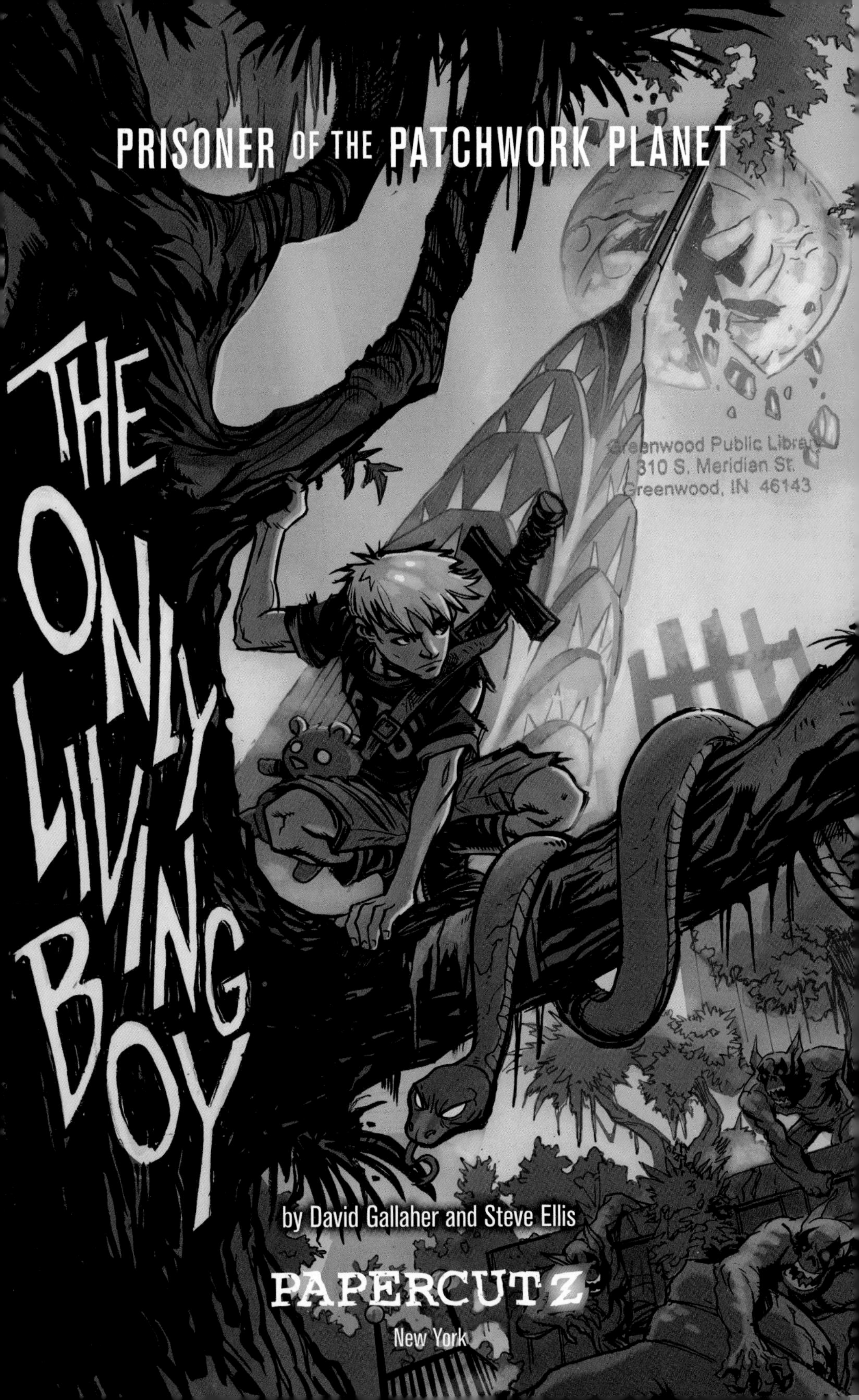

PRISONER OF THE PATCHWORK PLANET

THE ONLY LIVING BOY

by David Gallaher and Steve Ellis

PAPERCUTZ
New York

THE ONLY LIVING BOY #1 "Prisoner of the Patchwork Planet"

Dedicated to anyone who has felt lost and longed for greater adventures

Chapter 1
Writer/Co-Creator: David Gallaher
Artist/Co-Creator: Steve Ellis
Color Flatting: Mike Paar
Lettering: Scott O. Brown, Christy Sawyer

Chapter 2
Writer/Co-Creator: David Gallaher
Artist/Co-Creator: Steve Ellis
Color Flatting: Mike Paar, Ten Van Winkle
Lettering: April Brown, Scott O. Brown, Christy Sawyer

Originally serialized at: www.the-only-living-boy.com

Production – Dawn Guzzo
Production Coordinator – Jeff Whitman
Editor – Carol M. Burrell
Associate Editor – Bethany Bryan
Jim Salicrup
Editor-in-Chief

PB ISBN: 978-1-62991-442-8
HC ISBN: 978-1-62991-443-5

Printed in China February 2016 by Imago
2/F, Blk, 402, Cai Dian Industrial Zone
Huanggang North Road
Futian District, Shenzhen
China

Distributed by Macmillan
First Papercutz Printing

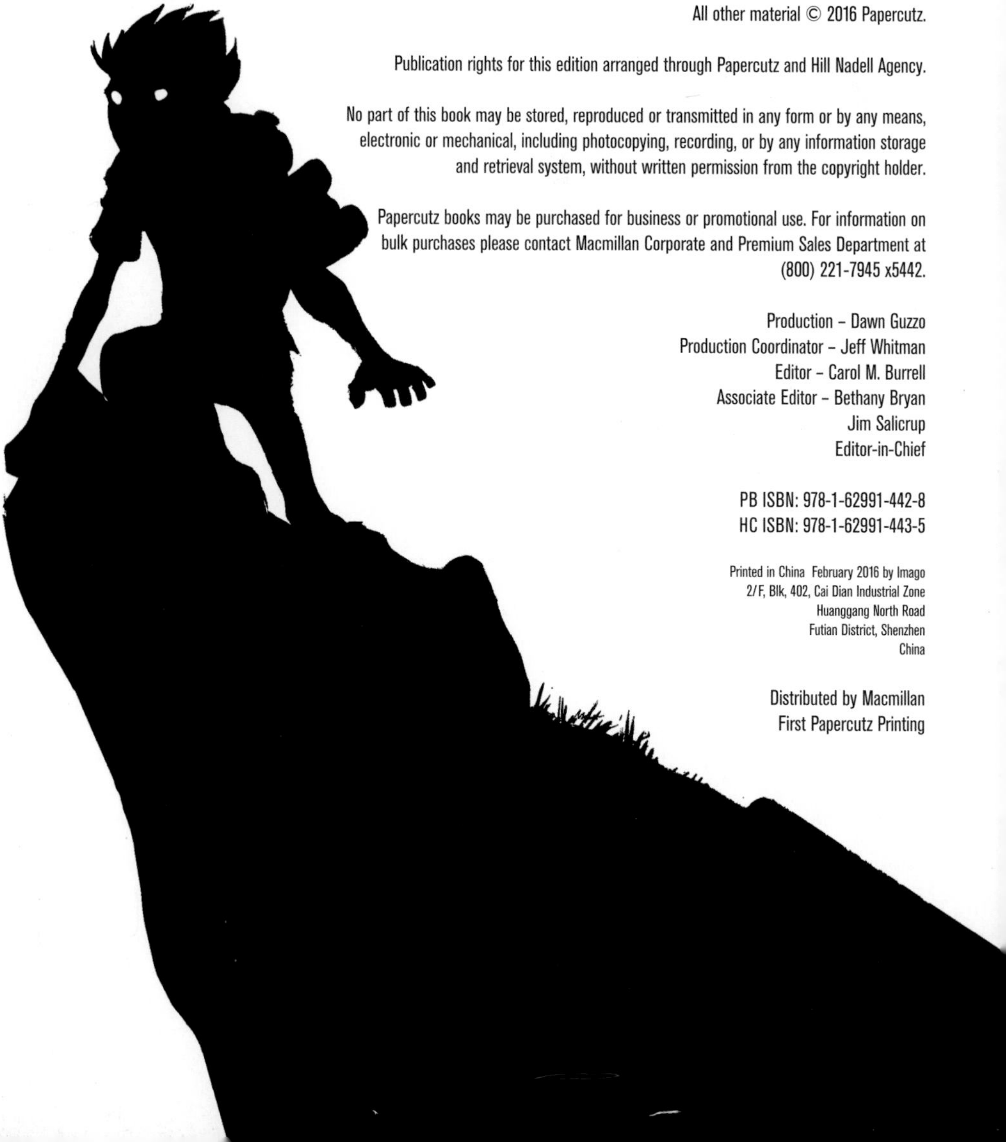

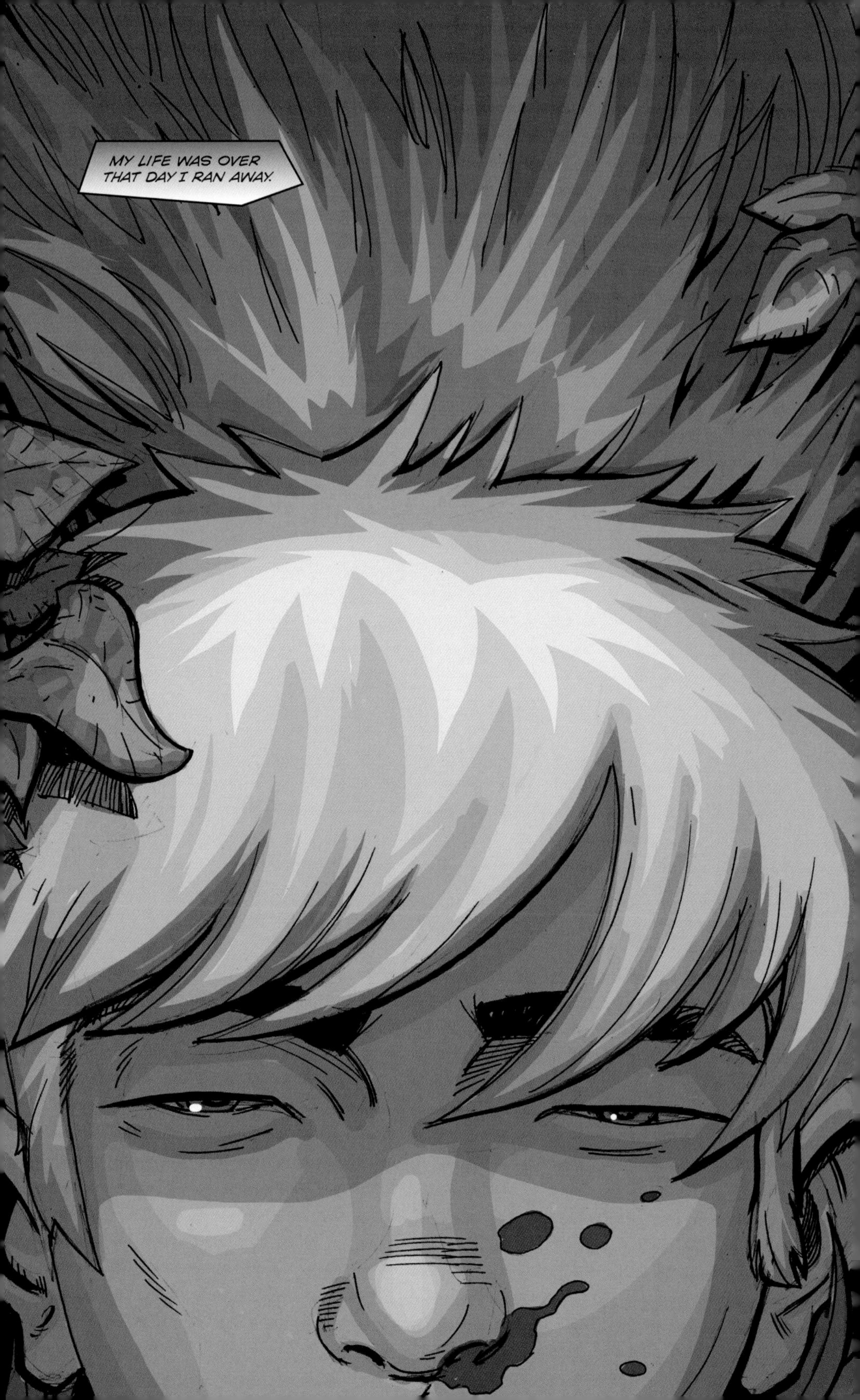
MY LIFE WAS OVER
THAT DAY I RAN AWAY.

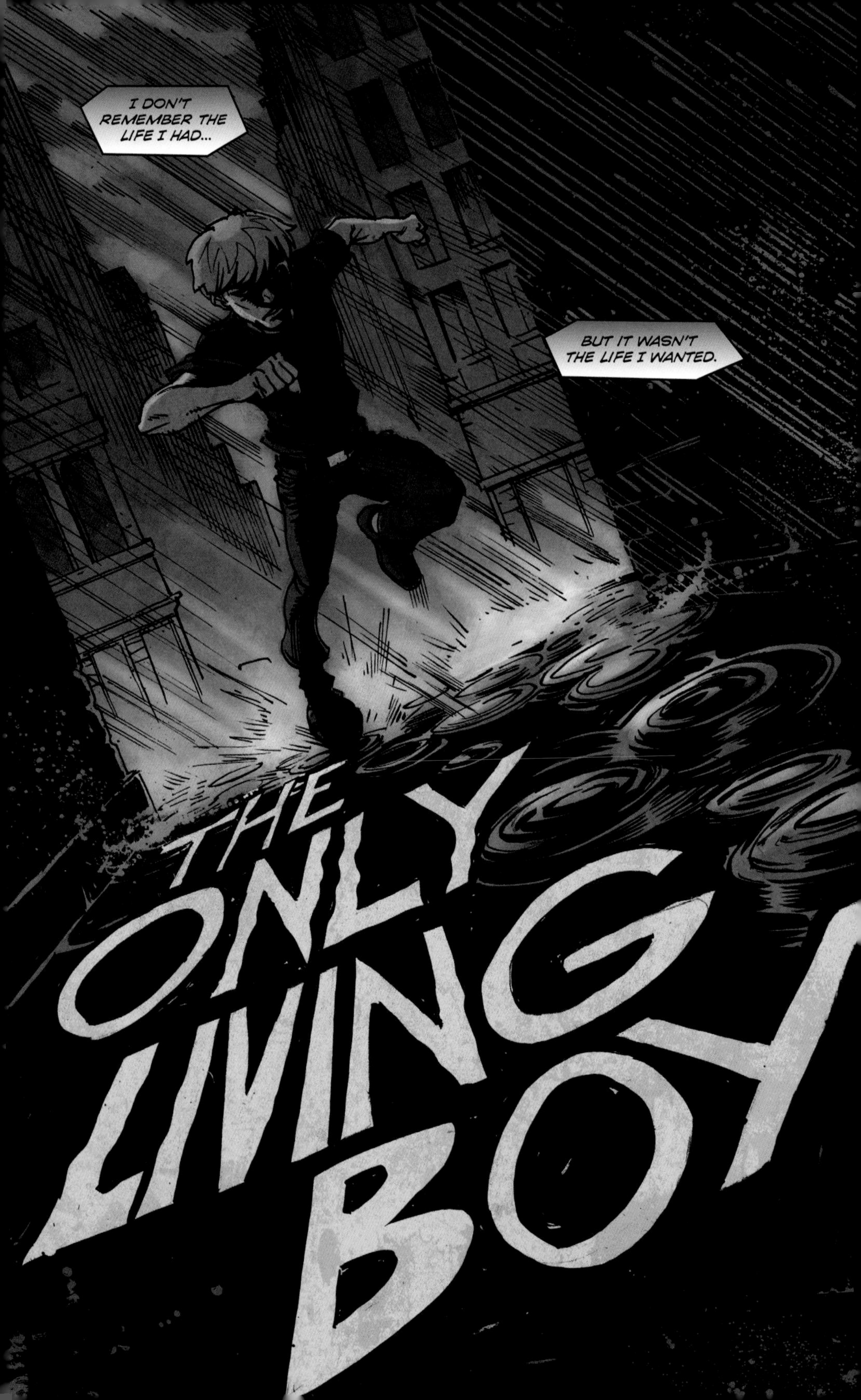
I DON'T REMEMBER THE LIFE I HAD...
BUT IT WASN'T THE LIFE I WANTED.
THE ONLY LIVING BOY

MY NAME IS
ERIK FARRELL.

I AM TWELVE
YEARS OLD.

I'M NOT SURE
RUNNING AWAY
WAS THE RIGHT
DECISION.

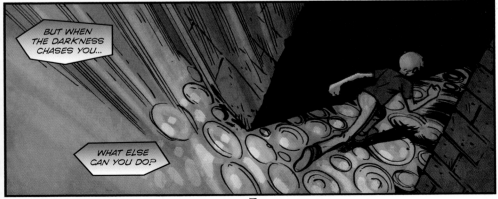

BUT WHEN
THE DARKNESS
CHASES YOU...

WHAT ELSE
CAN YOU DO?

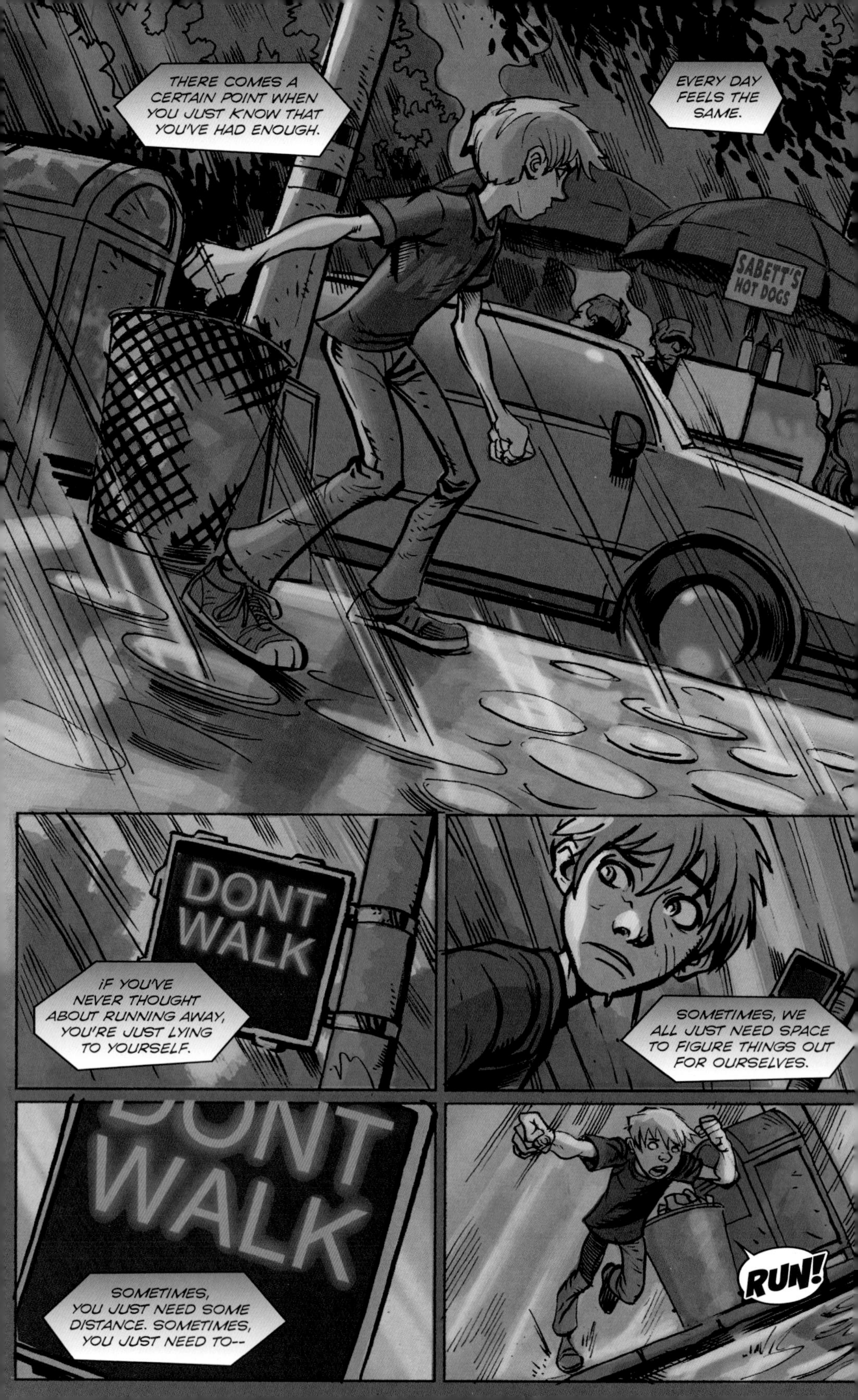

THERE COMES A CERTAIN POINT WHEN YOU JUST KNOW THAT YOU'VE HAD ENOUGH.
EVERY DAY FEELS THE SAME.
SABETT'S HOT DOGS
DONT WALK
iF YOU'VE NEVER THOUGHT ABOUT RUNNING AWAY, YOU'RE JUST LYING TO YOURSELF.
SOMETIMES, WE ALL JUST NEED SPACE TO FIGURE THINGS OUT FOR OURSELVES.
DONT WALK
SOMETIMES, YOU JUST NEED SOME DISTANCE. SOMETIMES, YOU JUST NEED TO--
RUN!

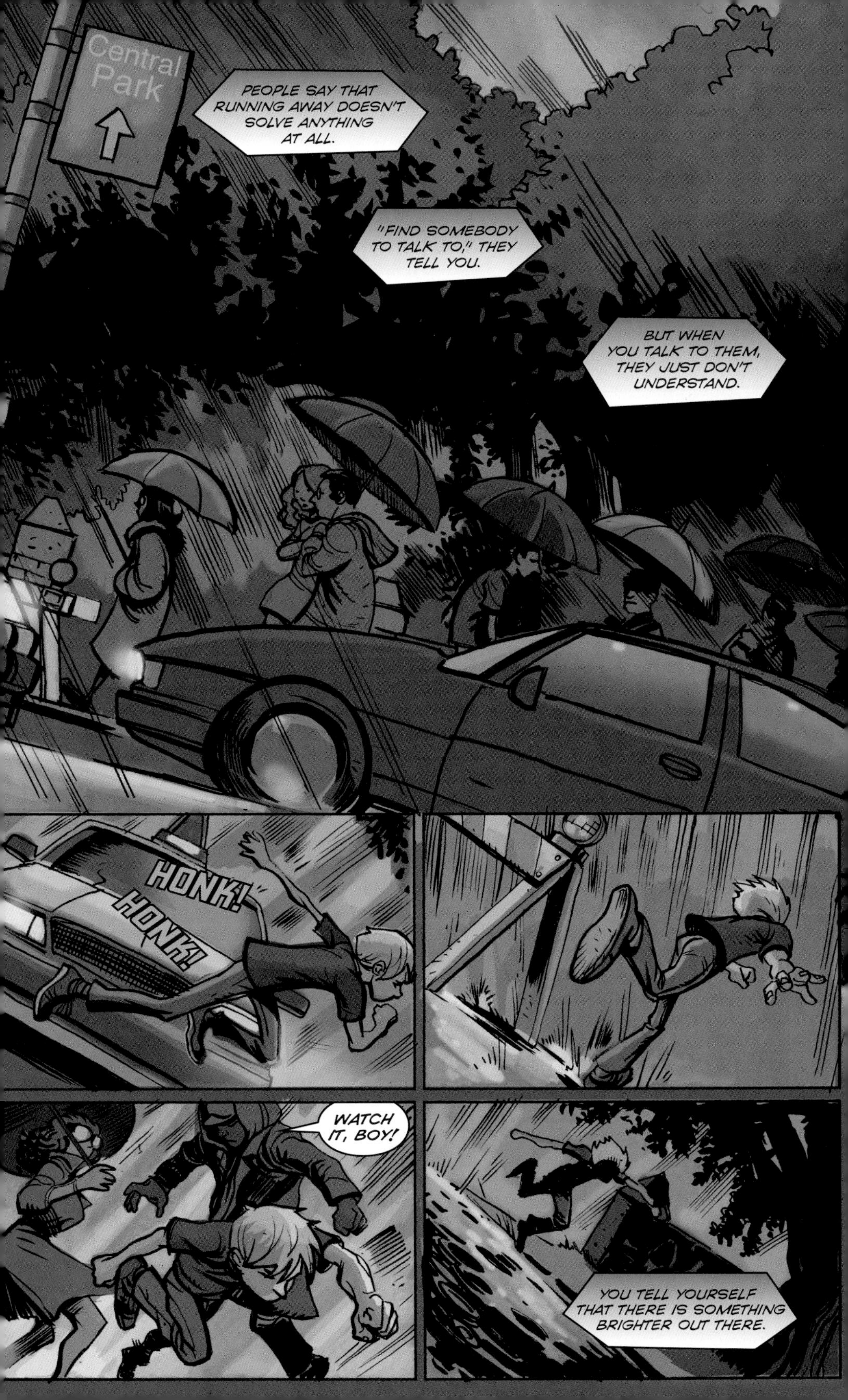
Central Park
PEOPLE SAY THAT RUNNING AWAY DOESN'T SOLVE ANYTHING AT ALL.
"FIND SOMEBODY TO TALK TO," THEY TELL YOU.
BUT WHEN YOU TALK TO THEM, THEY JUST DON'T UNDERSTAND.
HONK!
HONK!
WATCH IT, BOY!
YOU TELL YOURSELF THAT THERE IS SOMETHING BRIGHTER OUT THERE.

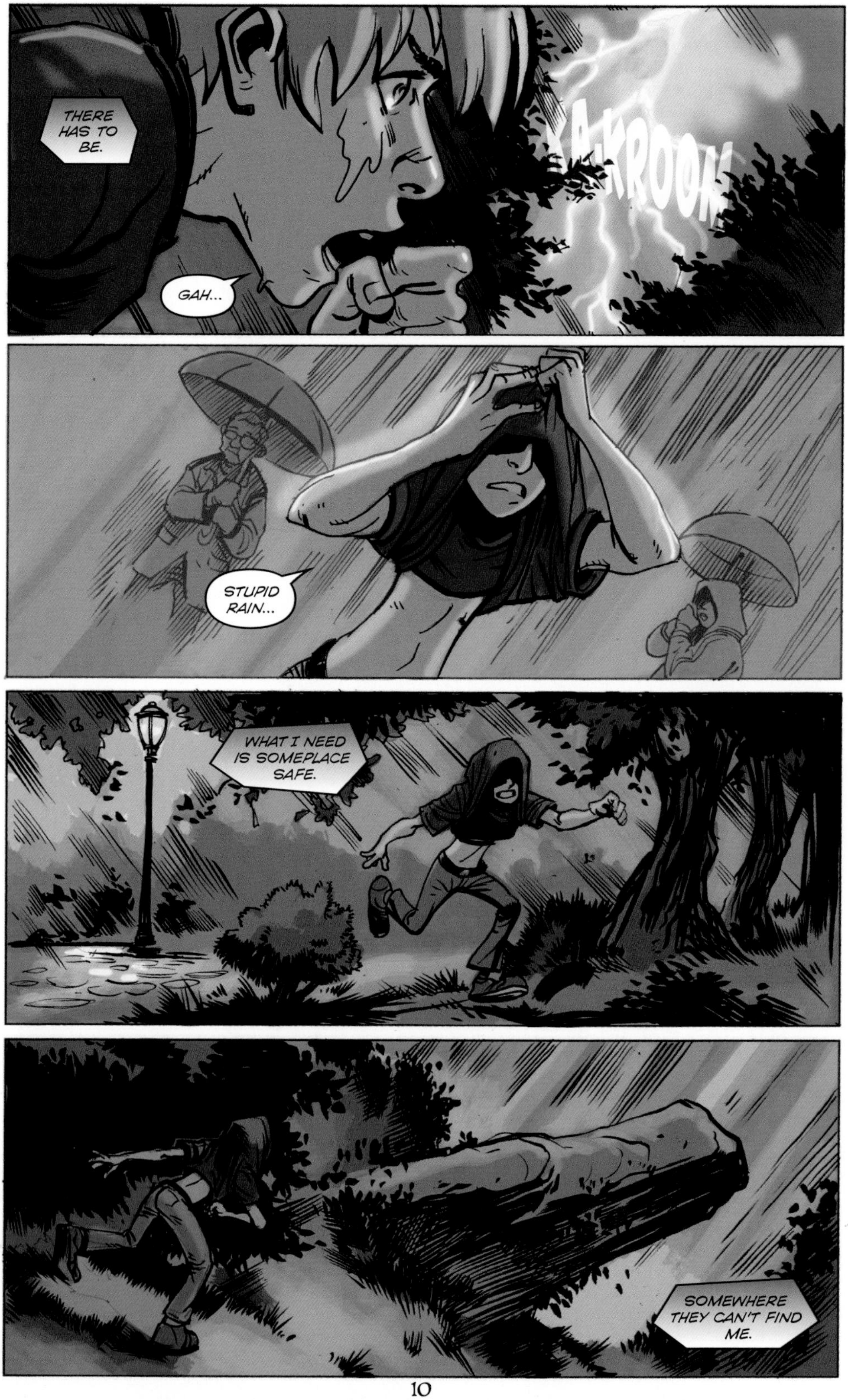
THERE HAS TO BE.
GAH...
STUPID RAIN...
WHAT I NEED IS SOMEPLACE SAFE.
SOMEWHERE THEY CAN'T FIND ME.

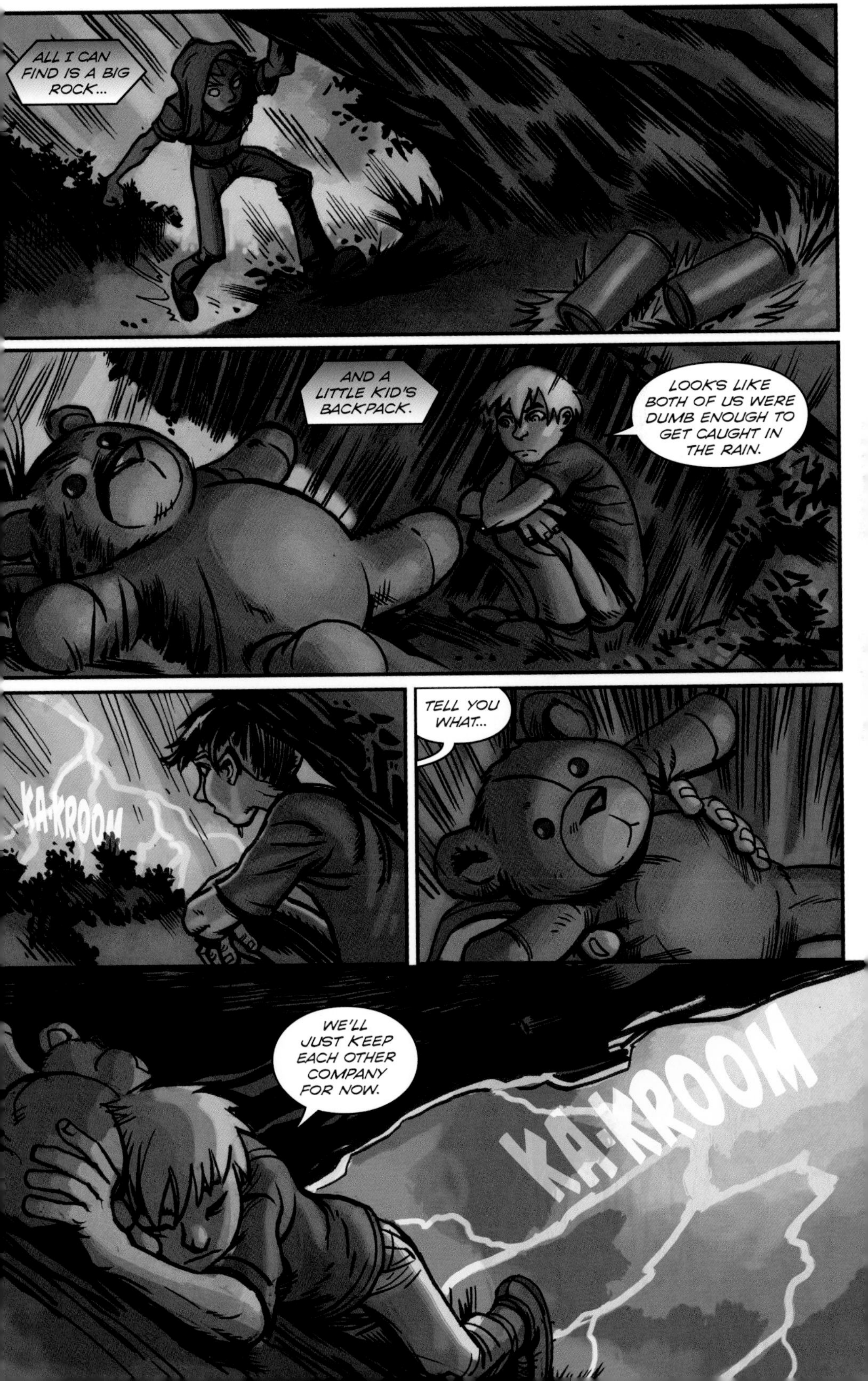
ALL I CAN FIND IS A BIG ROCK...
AND A LITTLE KID'S BACKPACK.
LOOKS LIKE BOTH OF US WERE DUMB ENOUGH TO GET CAUGHT IN THE RAIN.
KA-KROOM
TELL YOU WHAT...
WE'LL JUST KEEP EACH OTHER COMPANY FOR NOW.
KA-KROOM

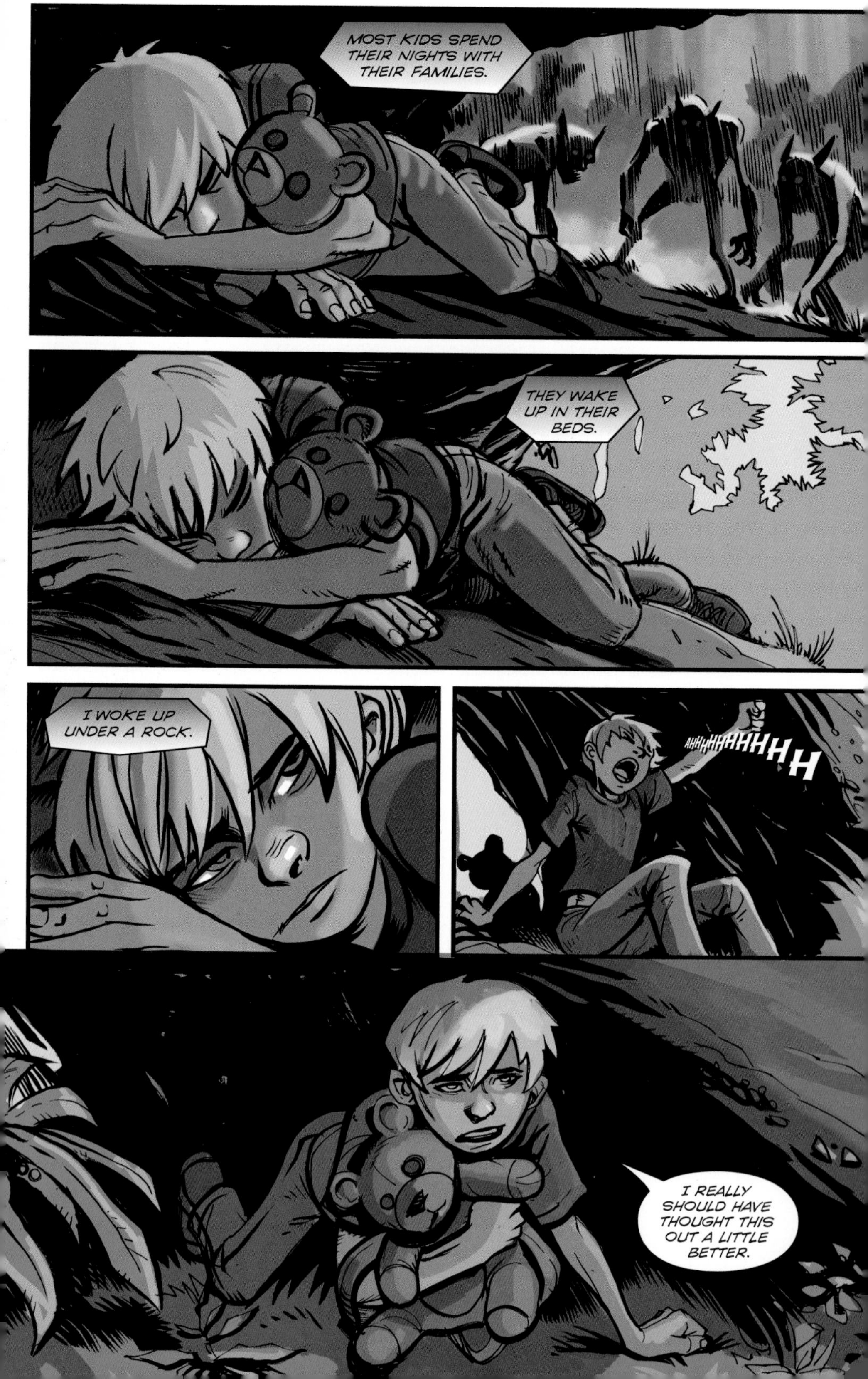
MOST KIDS SPEND THEIR NIGHTS WITH THEIR FAMILIES.
THEY WAKE UP IN THEIR BEDS.
I WOKE UP UNDER A ROCK.
AHHHHHHHHHHH
I REALLY SHOULD HAVE THOUGHT THIS OUT A LITTLE BETTER.

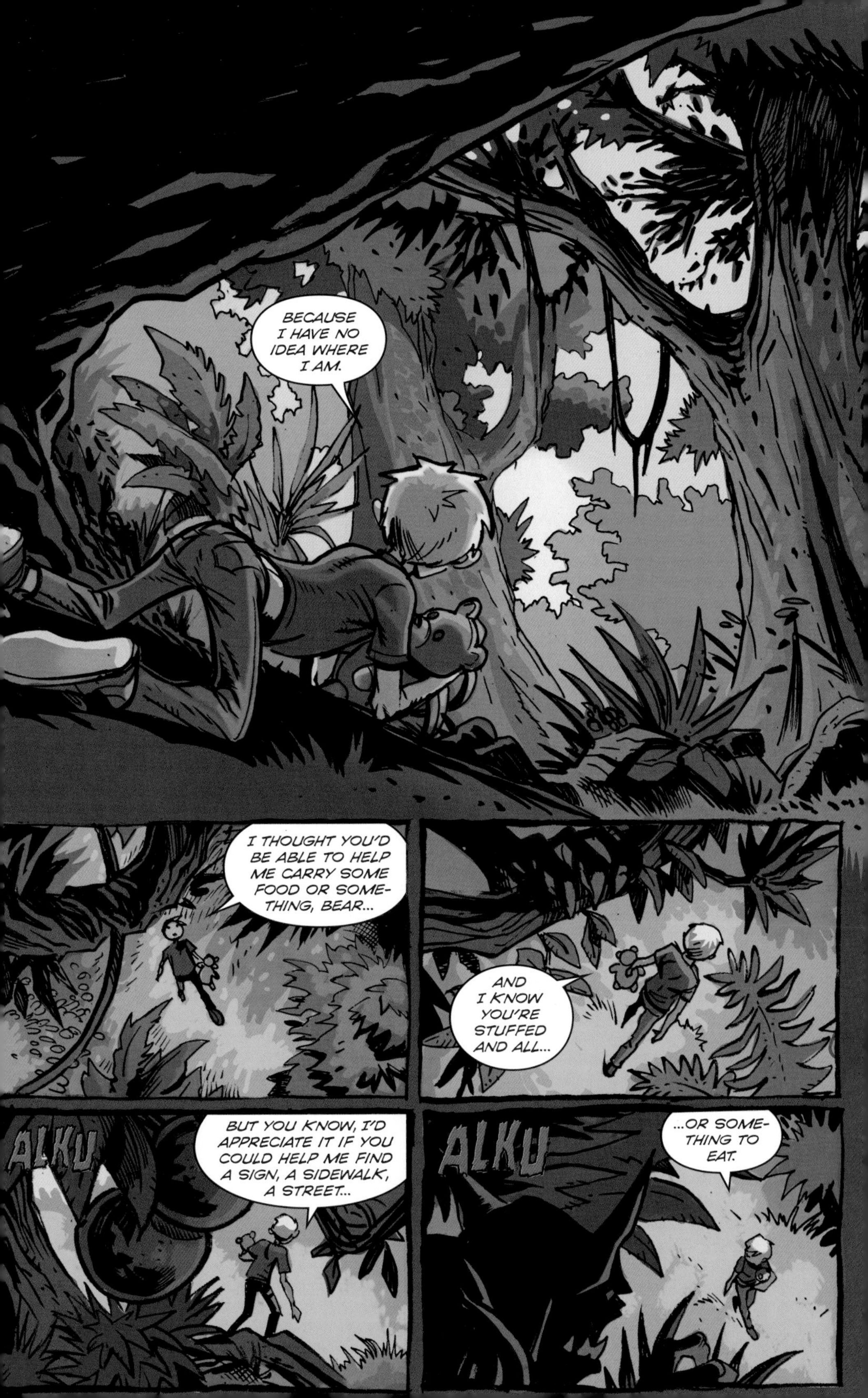
BECAUSE I HAVE NO IDEA WHERE I AM.
I THOUGHT YOU'D BE ABLE TO HELP ME CARRY SOME FOOD OR SOME-THING, BEAR...
AND I KNOW YOU'RE STUFFED AND ALL...
ALKU
BUT YOU KNOW, I'D APPRECIATE IT IF YOU COULD HELP ME FIND A SIGN, A SIDEWALK, A STREET...
ALKU
...OR SOME-THING TO EAT.

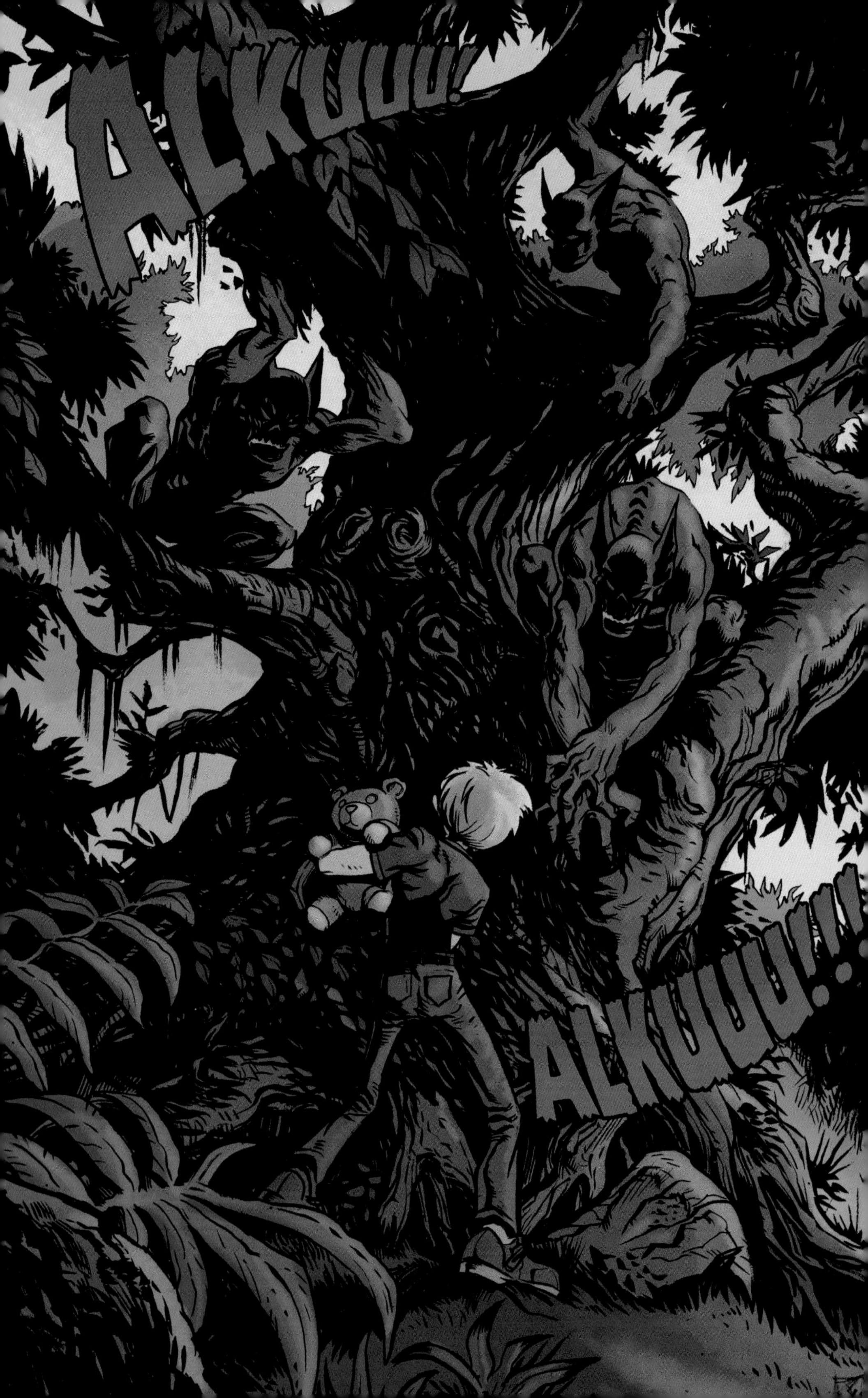
ALKUUU!
ALKUUU!!!

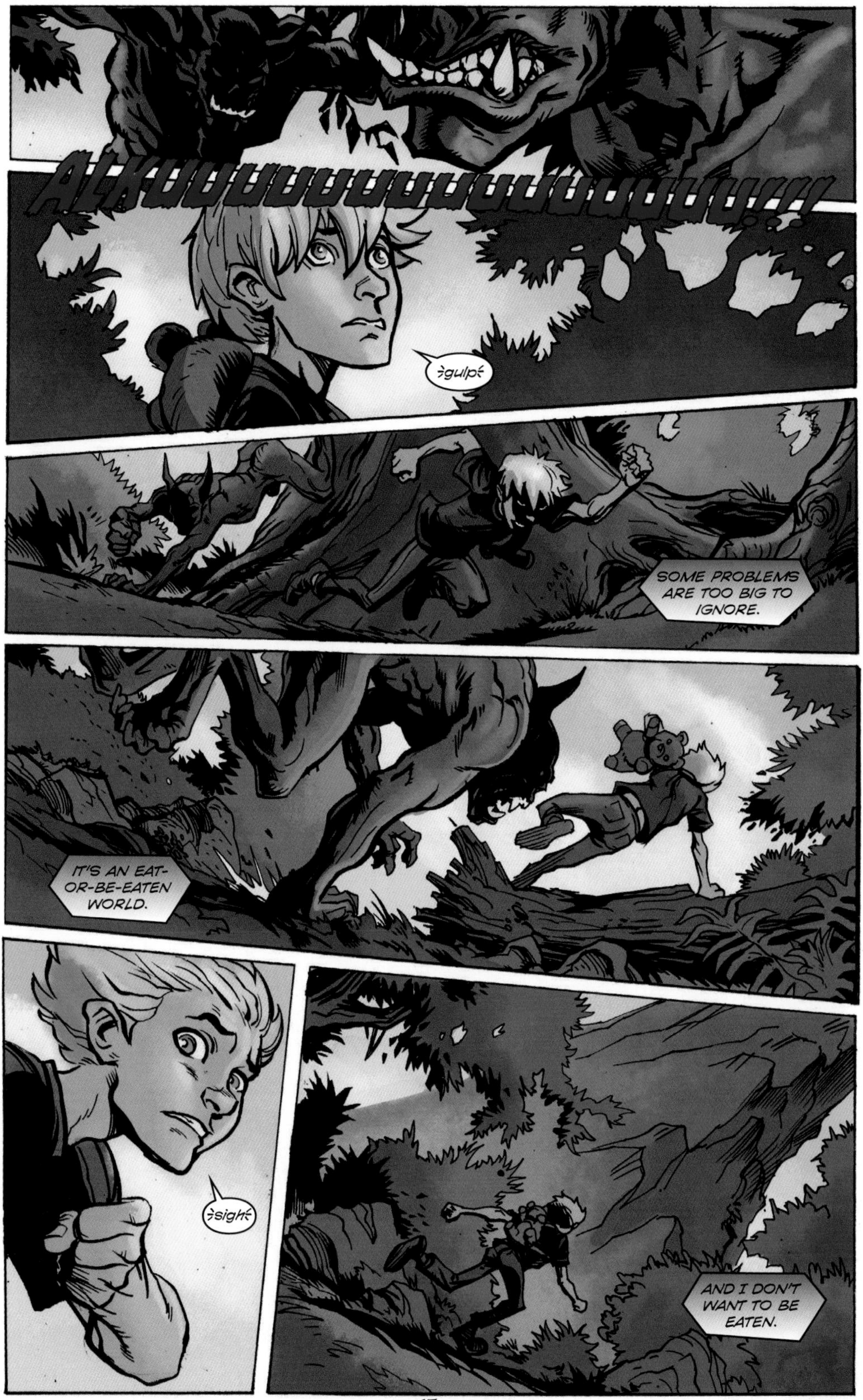
AKUUUUUUUUUUUUUUUU!!!
gulp
SOME PROBLEMS ARE TOO BIG TO IGNORE.
IT'S AN EAT-OR-BE-EATEN WORLD.
sigh
AND I DON'T WANT TO BE EATEN.

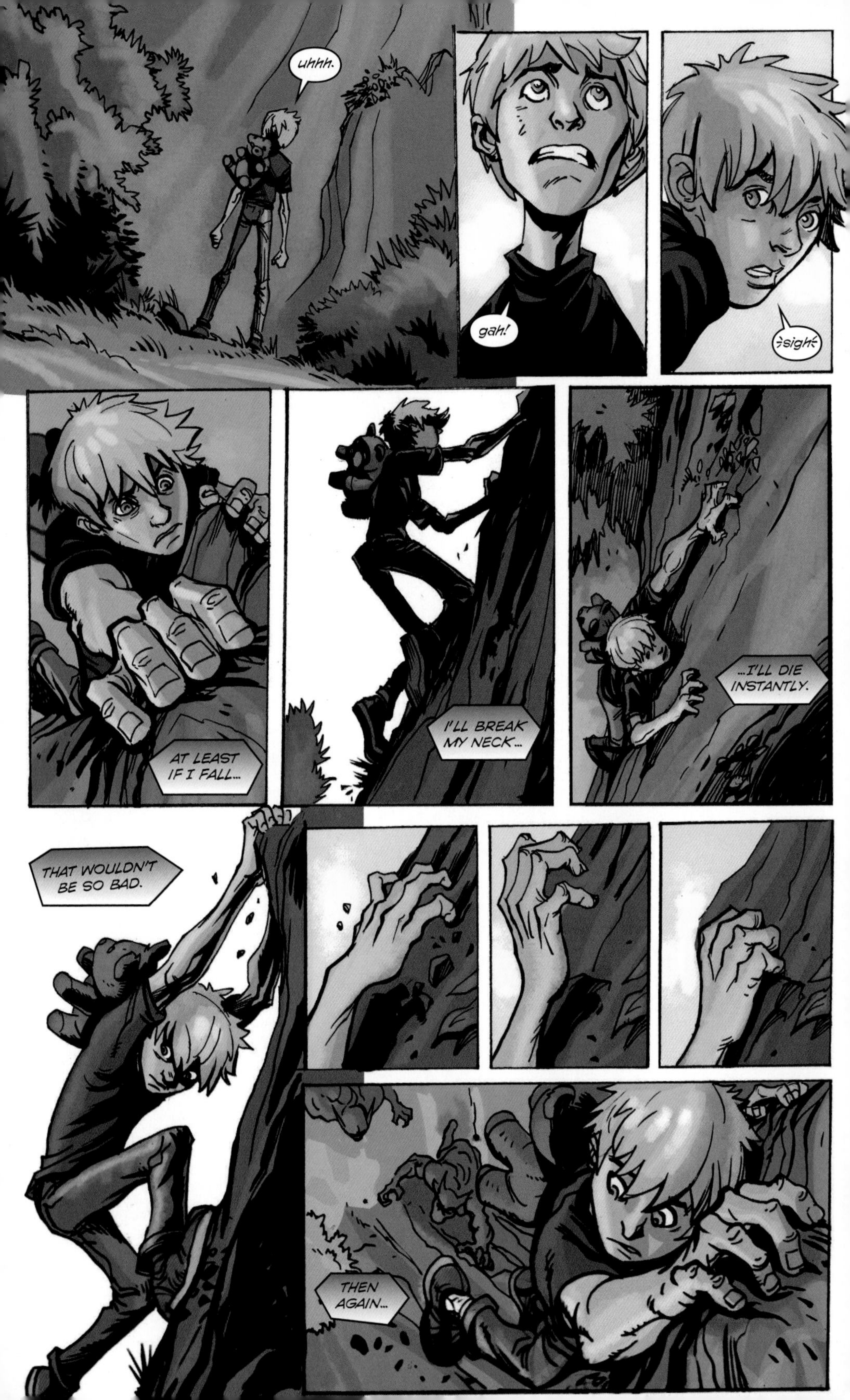
uhhh.
gah!
sigh
AT LEAST IF I FALL...
I'LL BREAK MY NECK...
...I'LL DIE INSTANTLY.
THAT WOULDN'T BE SO BAD.
THEN AGAIN...

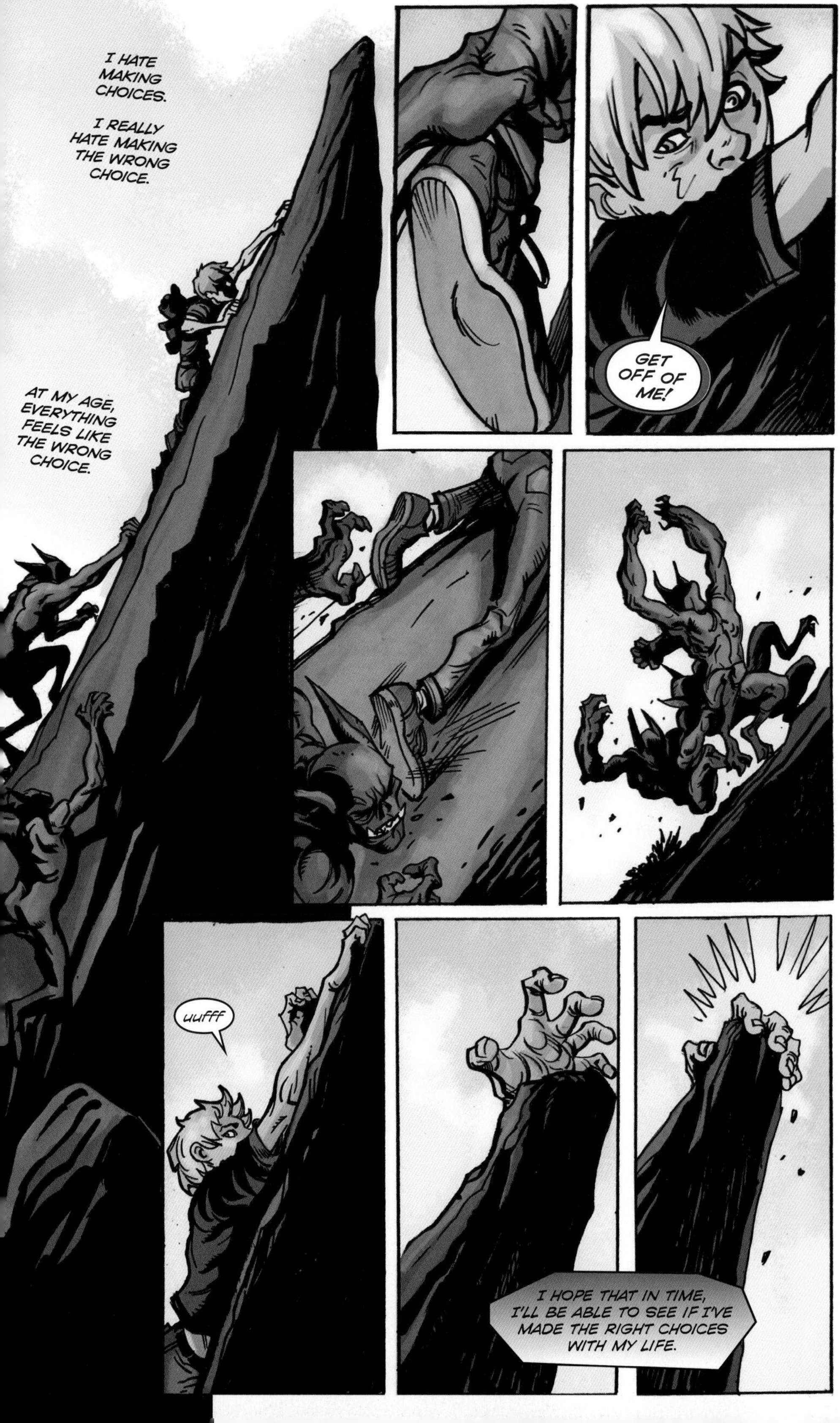
I HATE MAKING CHOICES.
I REALLY HATE MAKING THE WRONG CHOICE.
AT MY AGE, EVERYTHING FEELS LIKE THE WRONG CHOICE.
GET OFF OF ME!
uufff
I HOPE THAT IN TIME, I'LL BE ABLE TO SEE IF I'VE MADE THE RIGHT CHOICES WITH MY LIFE.

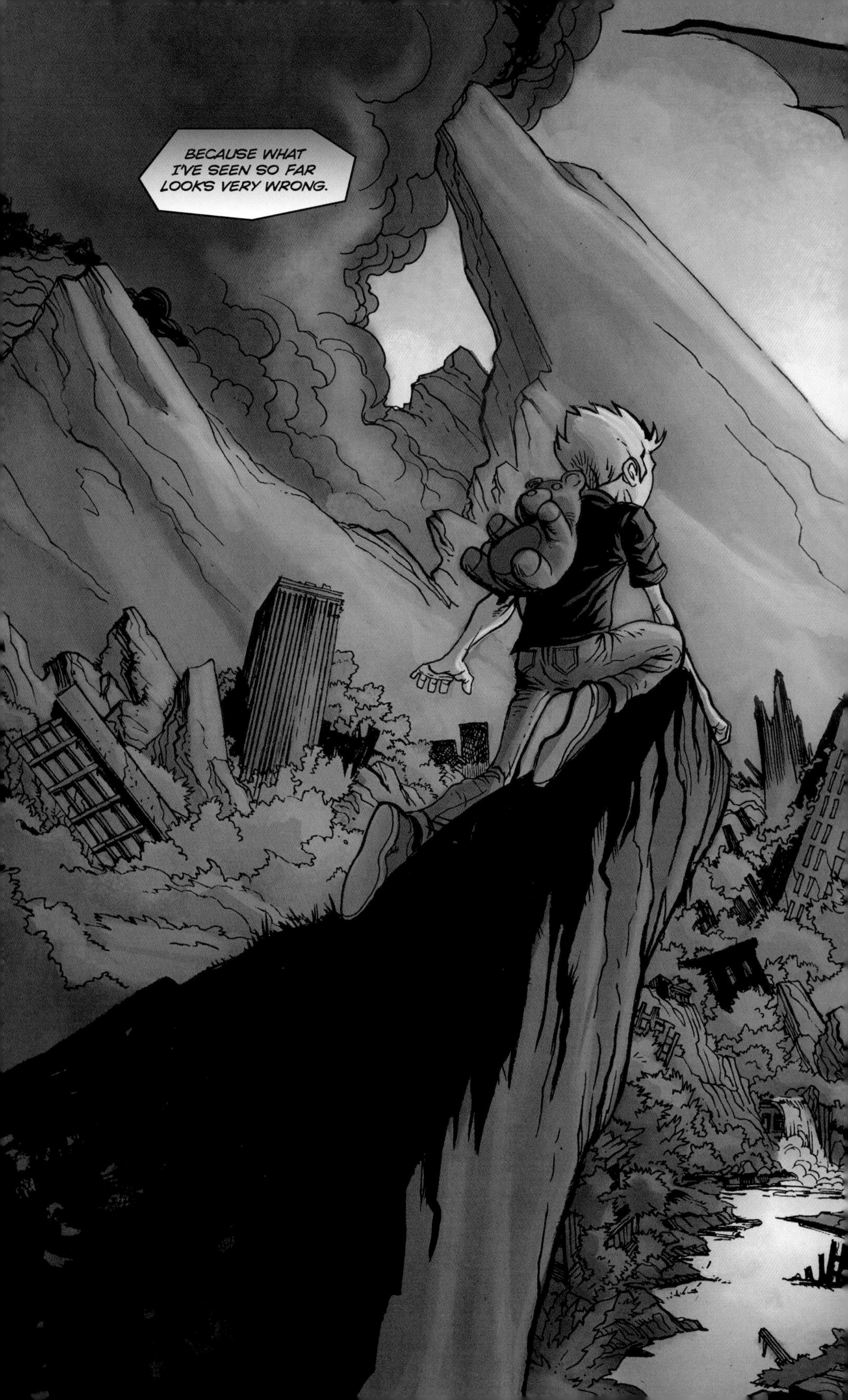
BECAUSE WHAT I'VE SEEN SO FAR LOOKS VERY WRONG.

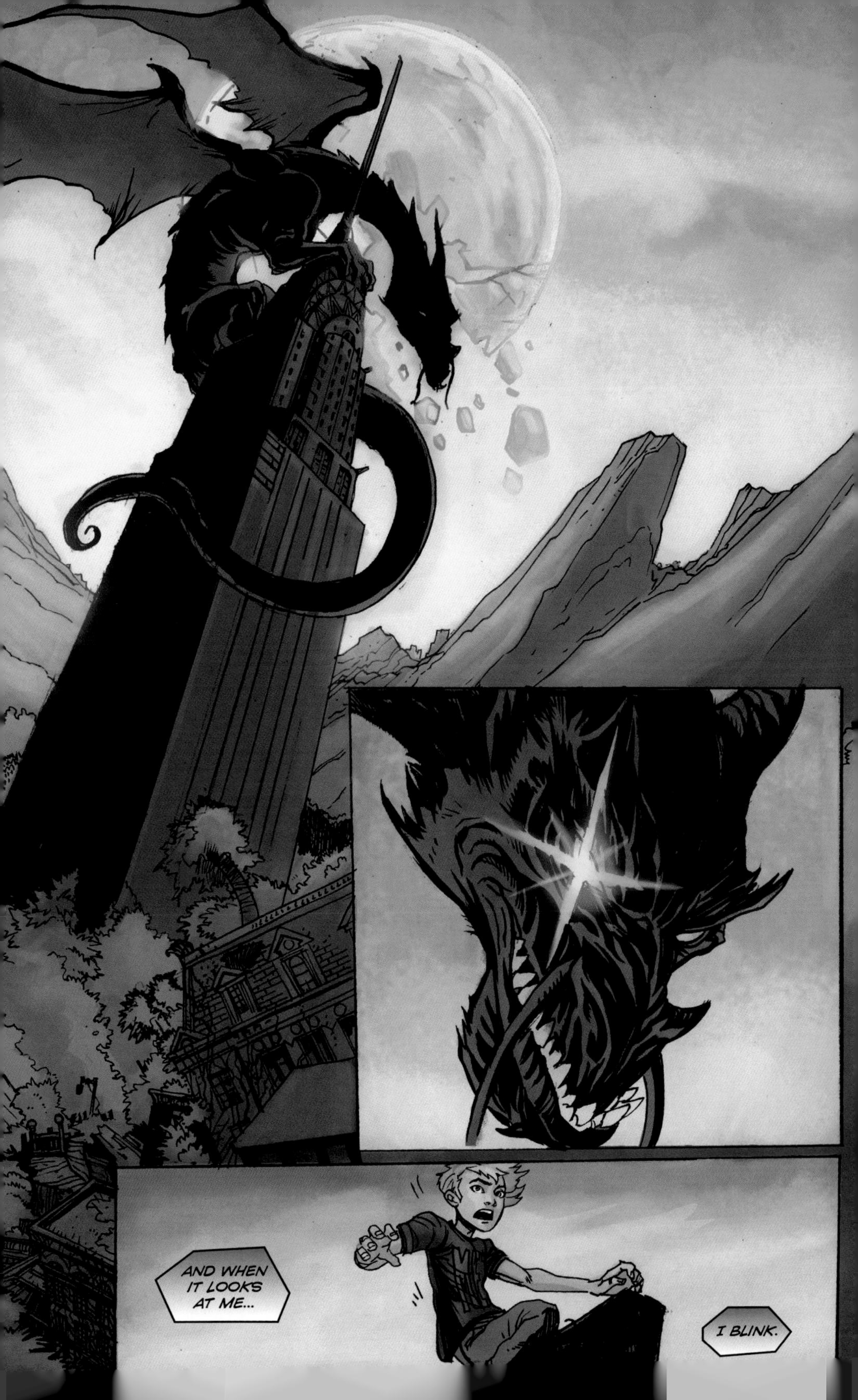
AND WHEN IT LOOKS AT ME...
I BLINK.

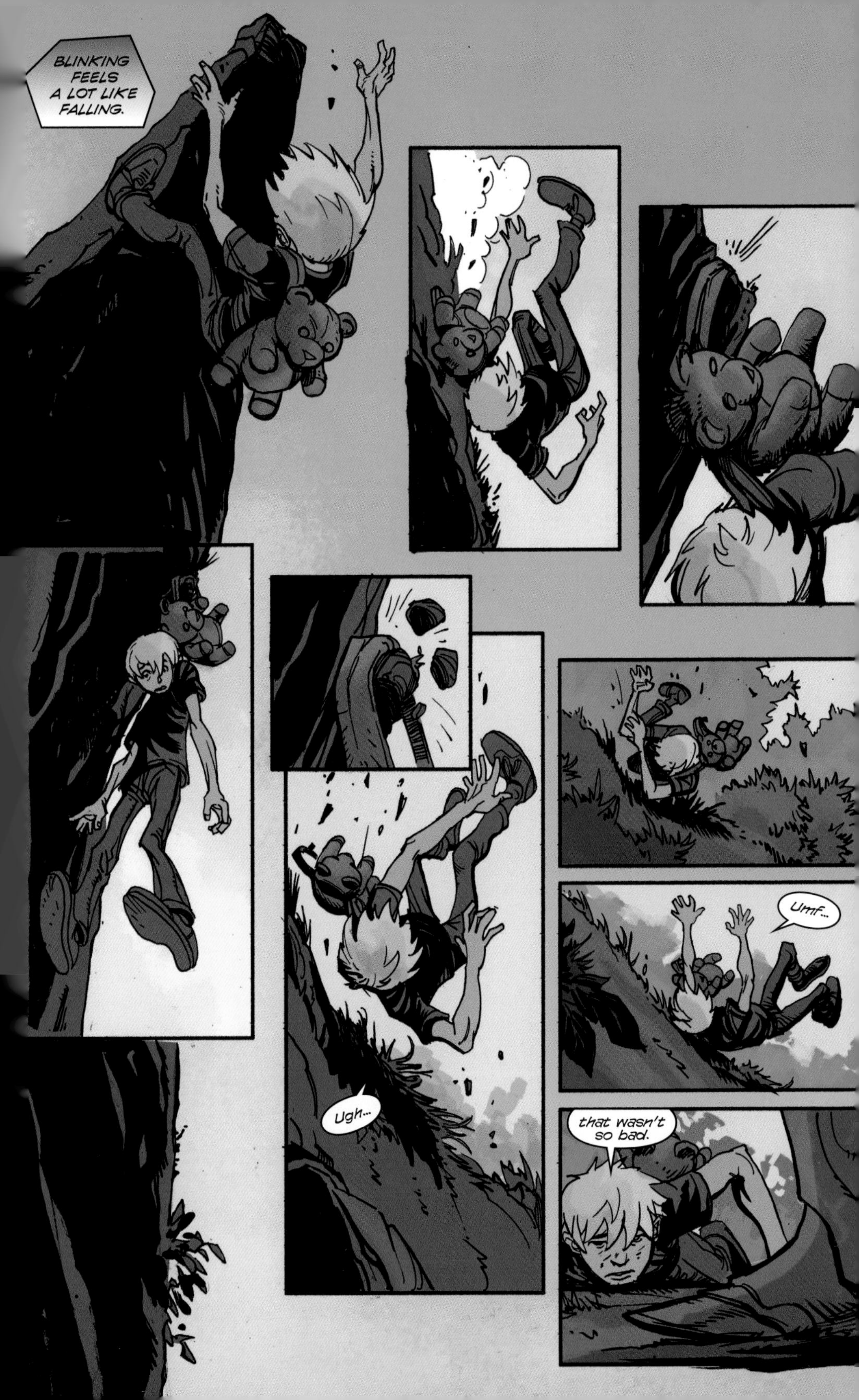
BLINKING FEELS A LOT LIKE FALLING.
Ugh...
Umf...
that wasn't so bad.

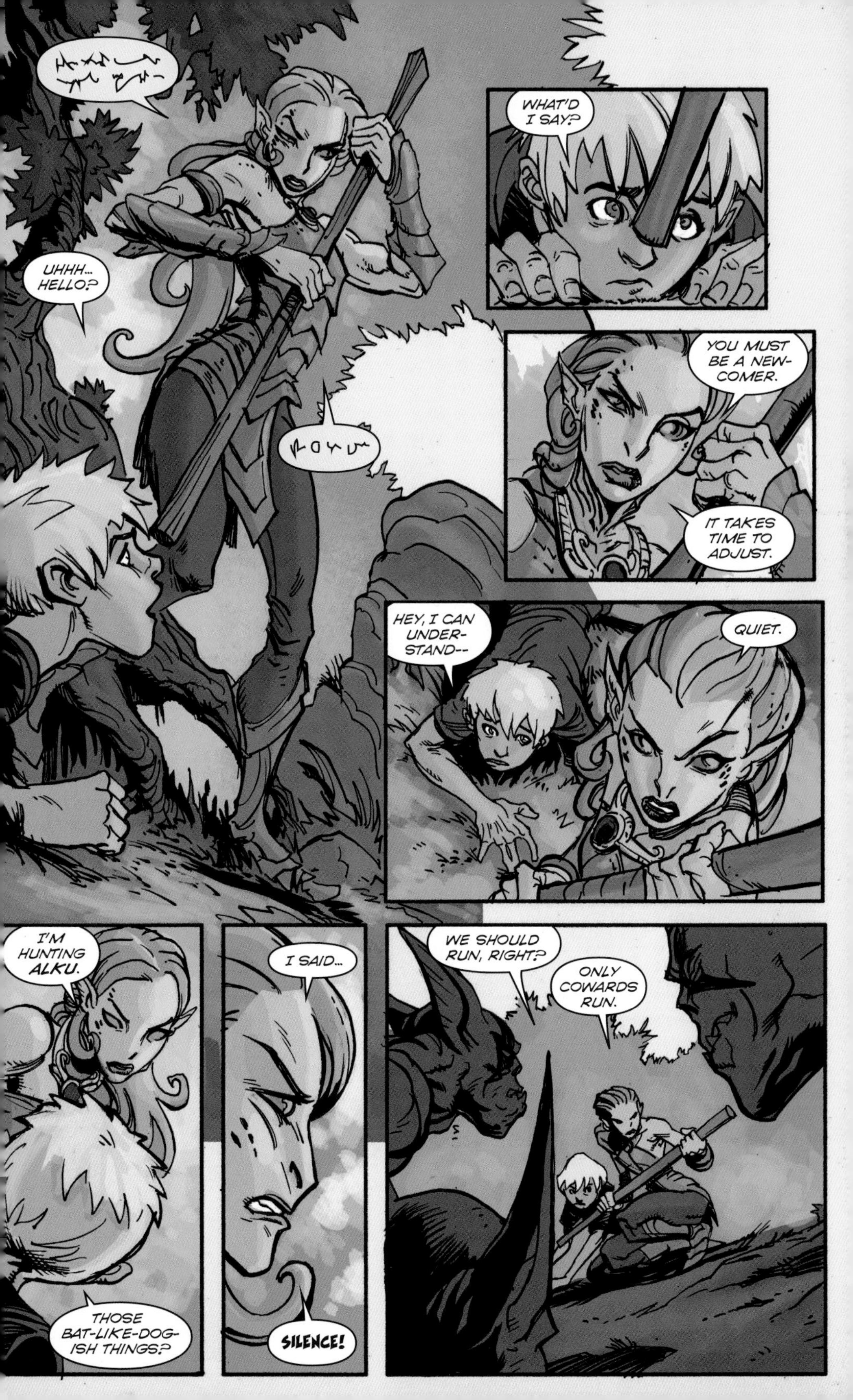
UHHH... HELLO?
WHAT'D I SAY?
YOU MUST BE A NEW-COMER.
IT TAKES TIME TO ADJUST.
HEY, I CAN UNDER-STAND--
QUIET.
I'M HUNTING ALKU.
THOSE BAT-LIKE-DOG-ISH THINGS?
I SAID...
SILENCE!
WE SHOULD RUN, RIGHT?
ONLY COWARDS RUN.

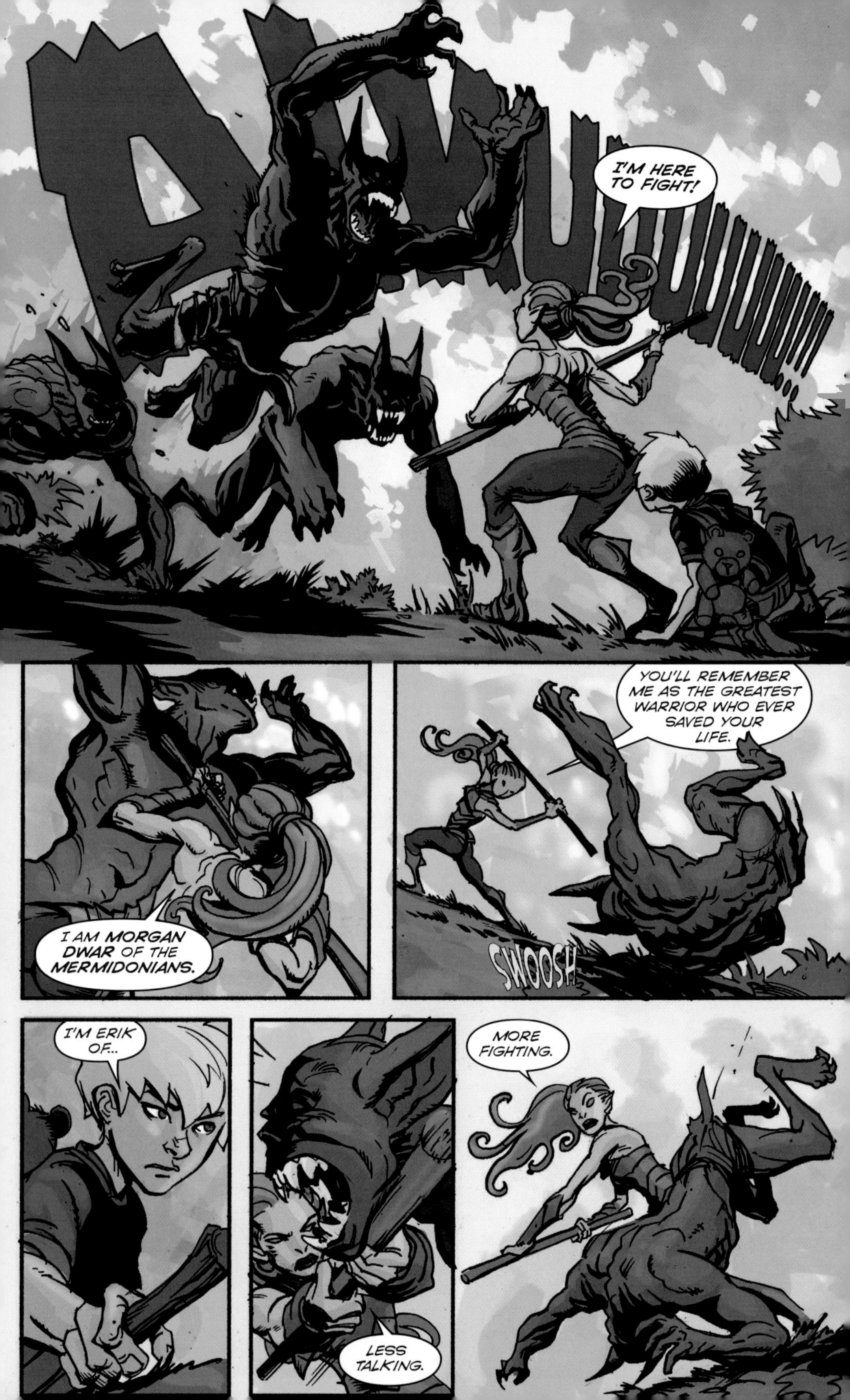
I'M HERE TO FIGHT!
I AM MORGAN DWAR OF THE MERMIDONIANS.
YOU'LL REMEMBER ME AS THE GREATEST WARRIOR WHO EVER SAVED YOUR LIFE.
SWOOSH
I'M ERIK OF...
LESS TALKING.
MORE FIGHTING.

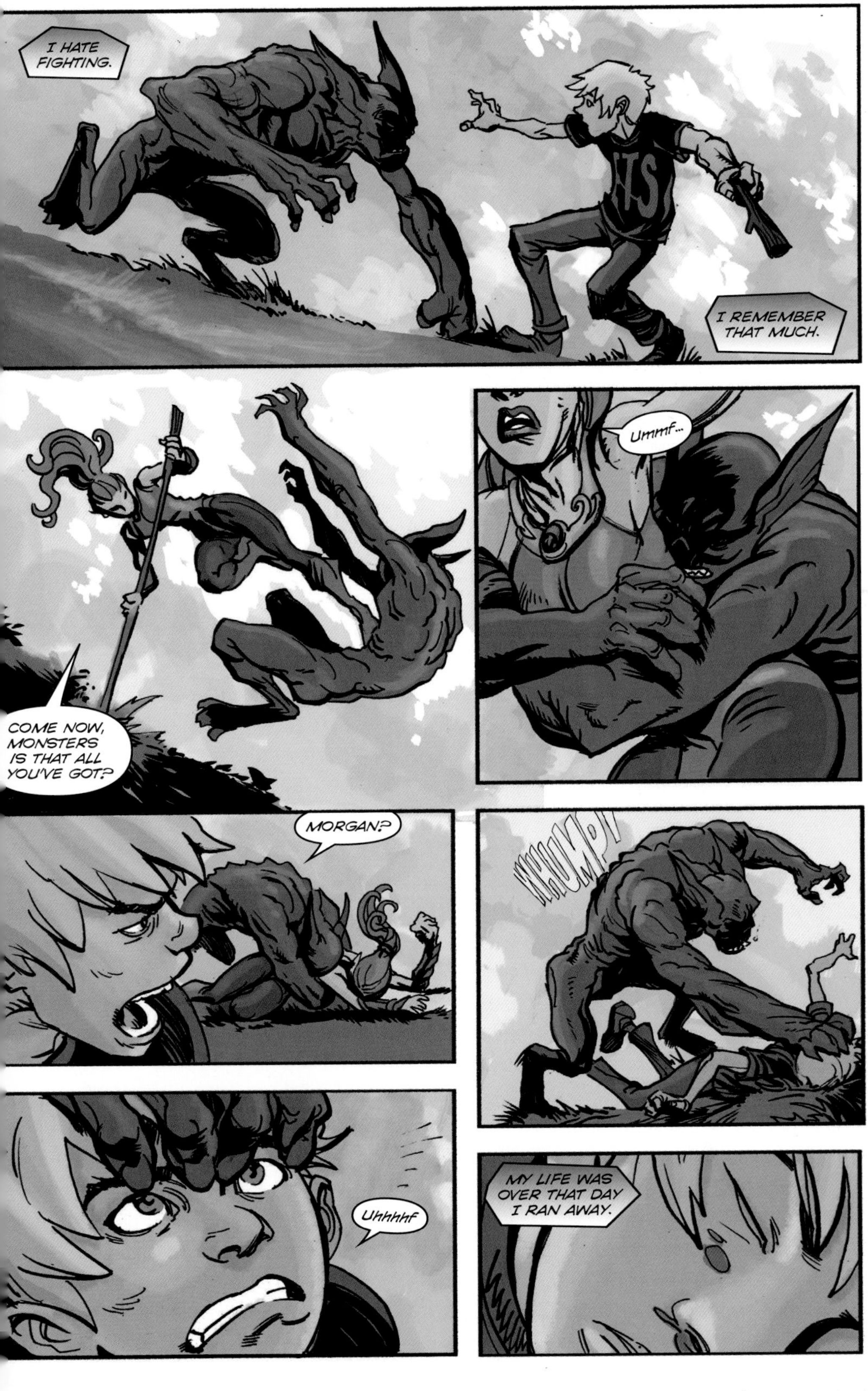
I HATE FIGHTING.
I REMEMBER THAT MUCH.
COME NOW, MONSTERS IS THAT ALL YOU'VE GOT?
Ummf...
MORGAN?
WHUMP!
Uhhhhf
MY LIFE WAS OVER THAT DAY I RAN AWAY.

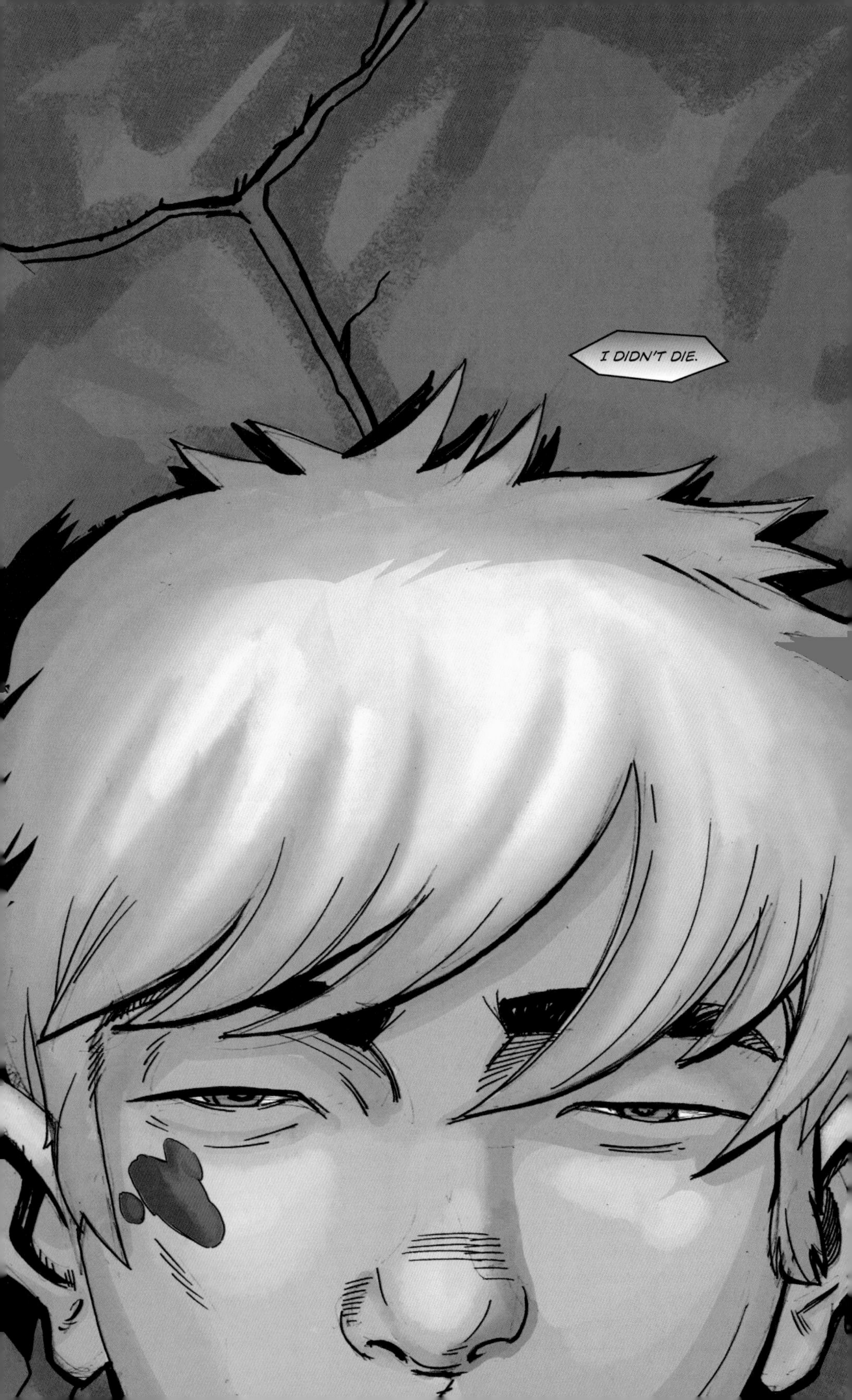
I DIDN'T DIE.

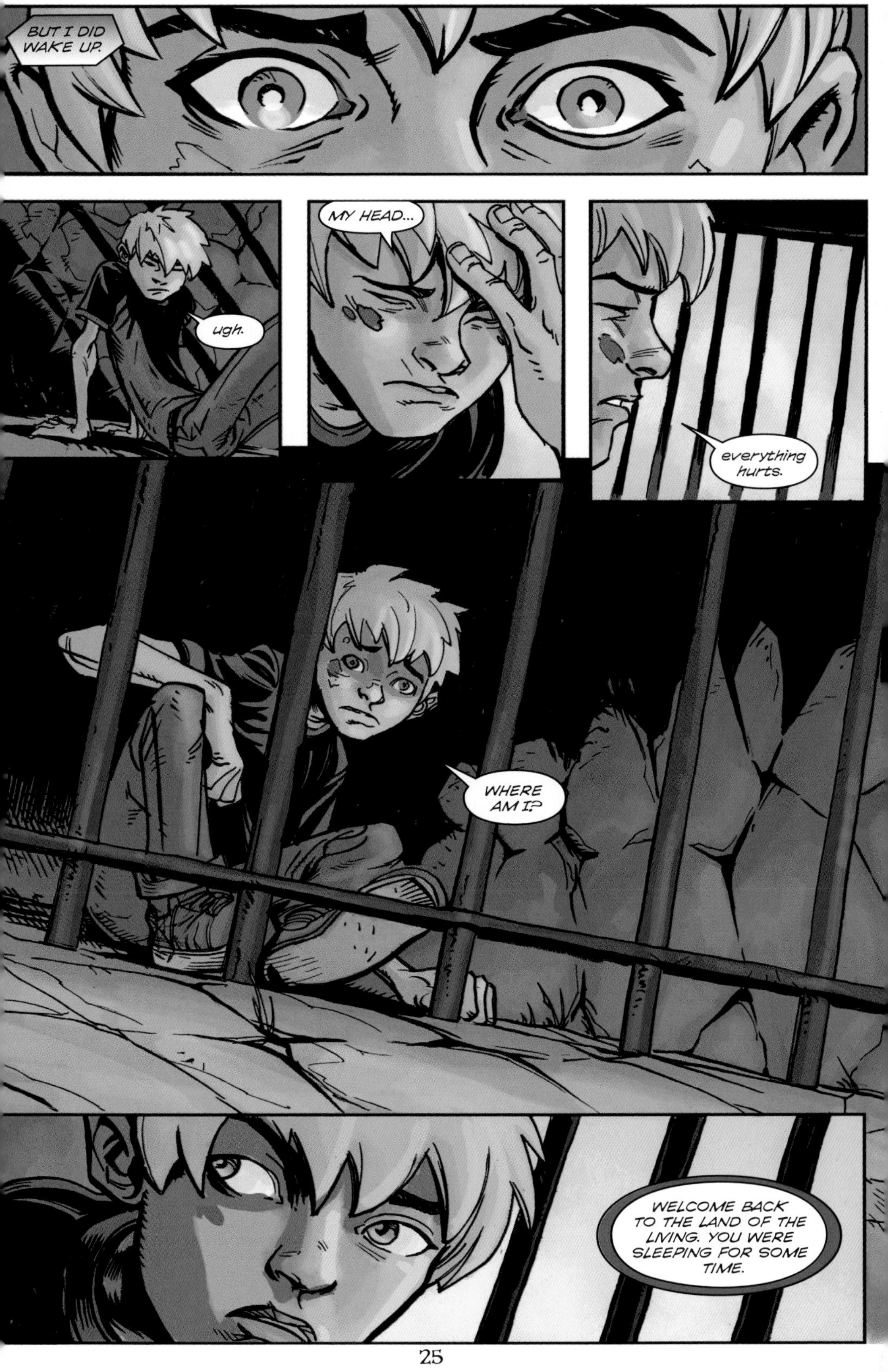
BUT I DID WAKE UP.
ugh.
MY HEAD...
everything hurts.
WHERE AM I?
WELCOME BACK TO THE LAND OF THE LIVING. YOU WERE SLEEPING FOR SOME TIME.

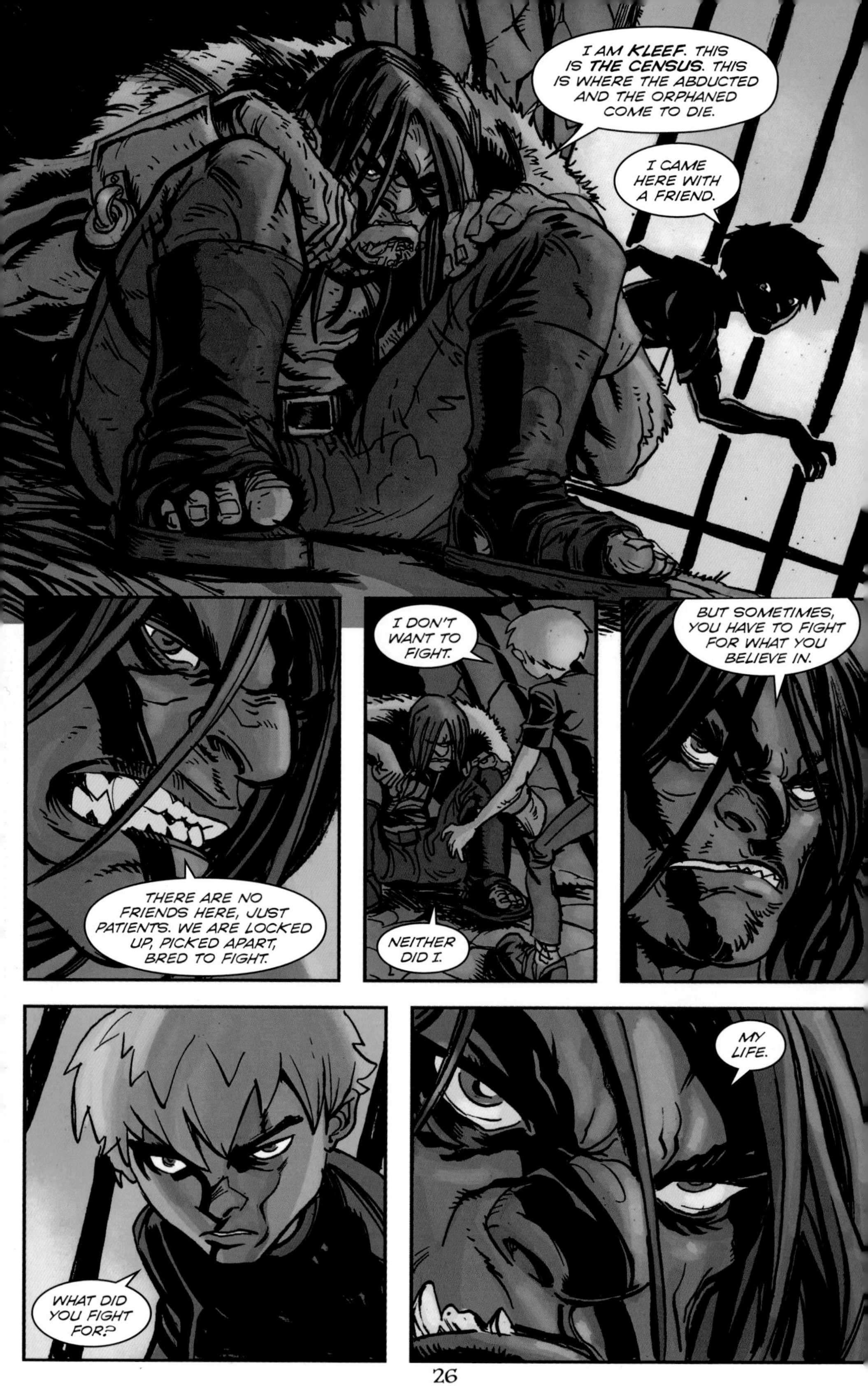
I AM KLEEF. THIS IS THE CENSUS. THIS IS WHERE THE ABDUCTED AND THE ORPHANED COME TO DIE.
I CAME HERE WITH A FRIEND.
THERE ARE NO FRIENDS HERE, JUST PATIENTS. WE ARE LOCKED UP, PICKED APART, BRED TO FIGHT.
I DON'T WANT TO FIGHT.
NEITHER DID I.
BUT SOMETIMES, YOU HAVE TO FIGHT FOR WHAT YOU BELIEVE IN.
WHAT DID YOU FIGHT FOR?
MY LIFE.

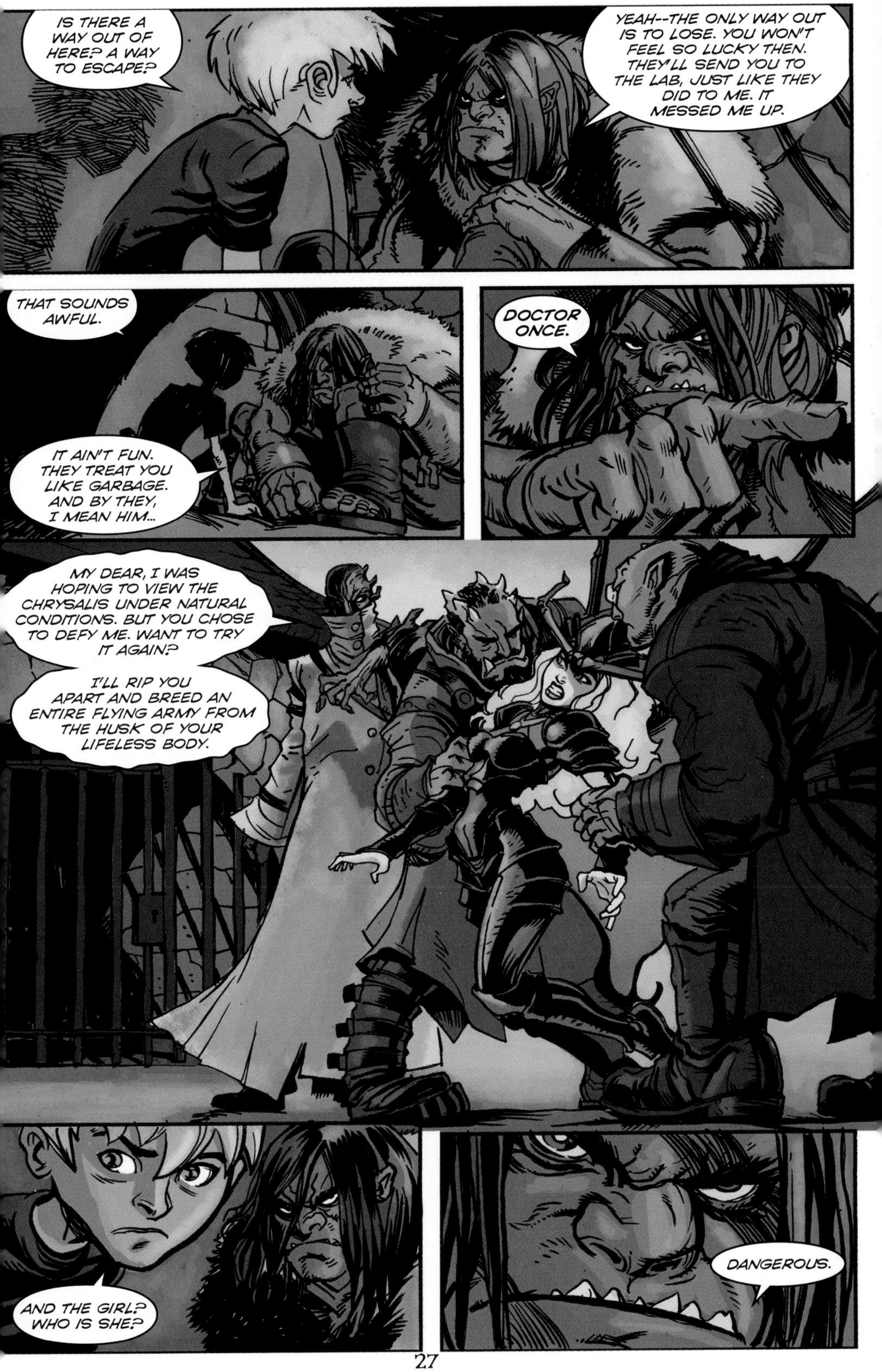
IS THERE A WAY OUT OF HERE? A WAY TO ESCAPE?
YEAH--THE ONLY WAY OUT IS TO LOSE. YOU WON'T FEEL SO LUCKY THEN. THEY'LL SEND YOU TO THE LAB, JUST LIKE THEY DID TO ME. IT MESSED ME UP.
THAT SOUNDS AWFUL.
IT AIN'T FUN. THEY TREAT YOU LIKE GARBAGE. AND BY THEY, I MEAN HIM...
DOCTOR ONCE.
MY DEAR, I WAS HOPING TO VIEW THE CHRYSALIS UNDER NATURAL CONDITIONS. BUT YOU CHOSE TO DEFY ME. WANT TO TRY IT AGAIN?
I'LL RIP YOU APART AND BREED AN ENTIRE FLYING ARMY FROM THE HUSK OF YOUR LIFELESS BODY.
AND THE GIRL? WHO IS SHE?
DANGEROUS.

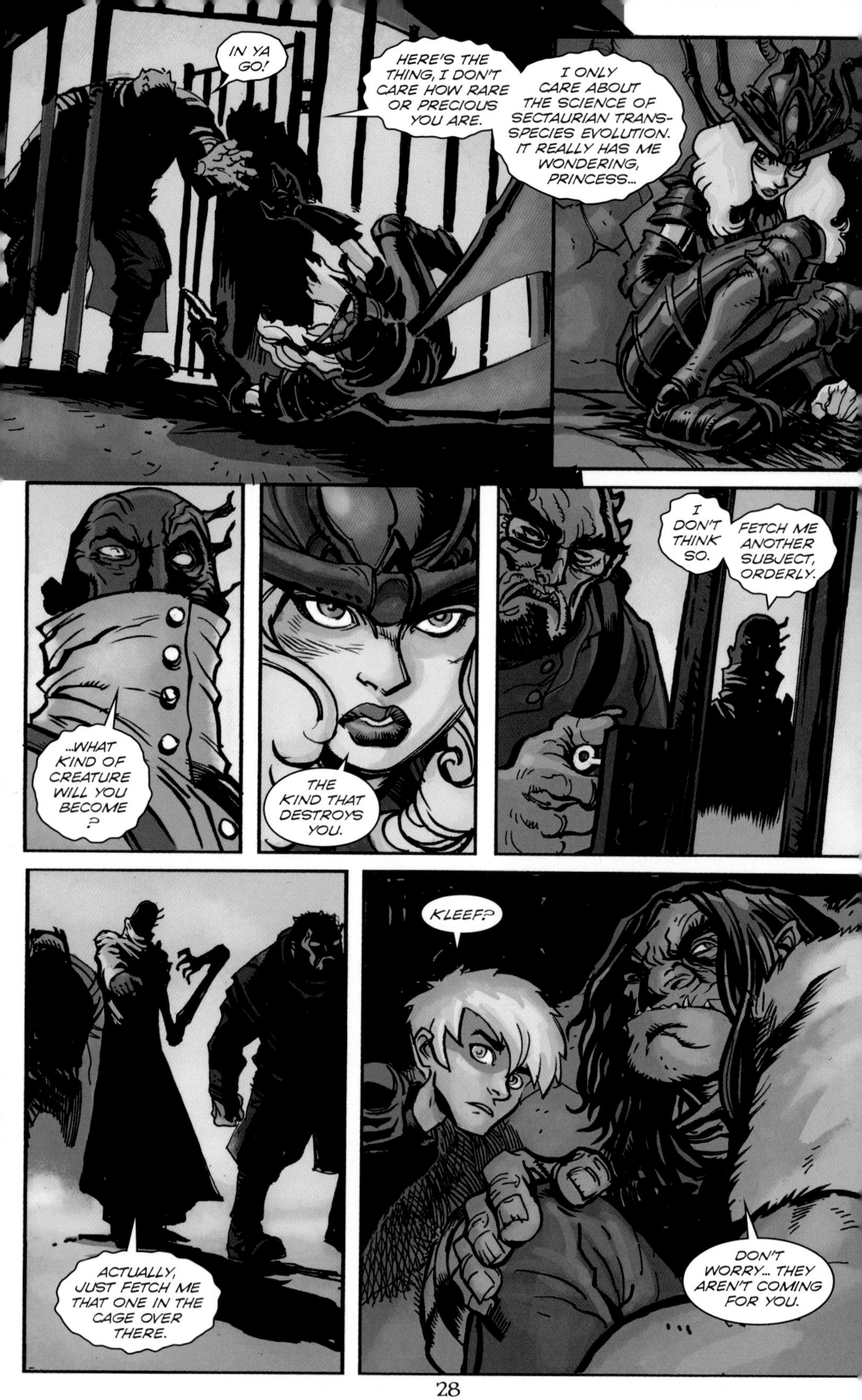
IN YA GO!
HERE'S THE THING, I DON'T CARE HOW RARE OR PRECIOUS YOU ARE.
I ONLY CARE ABOUT THE SCIENCE OF SECTAURIAN TRANS-SPECIES EVOLUTION. IT REALLY HAS ME WONDERING, PRINCESS...
...WHAT KIND OF CREATURE WILL YOU BECOME?
THE KIND THAT DESTROYS YOU.
I DON'T THINK SO.
FETCH ME ANOTHER SUBJECT, ORDERLY.
ACTUALLY, JUST FETCH ME THAT ONE IN THE CAGE OVER THERE.
KLEEF?
DON'T WORRY... THEY AREN'T COMING FOR YOU.

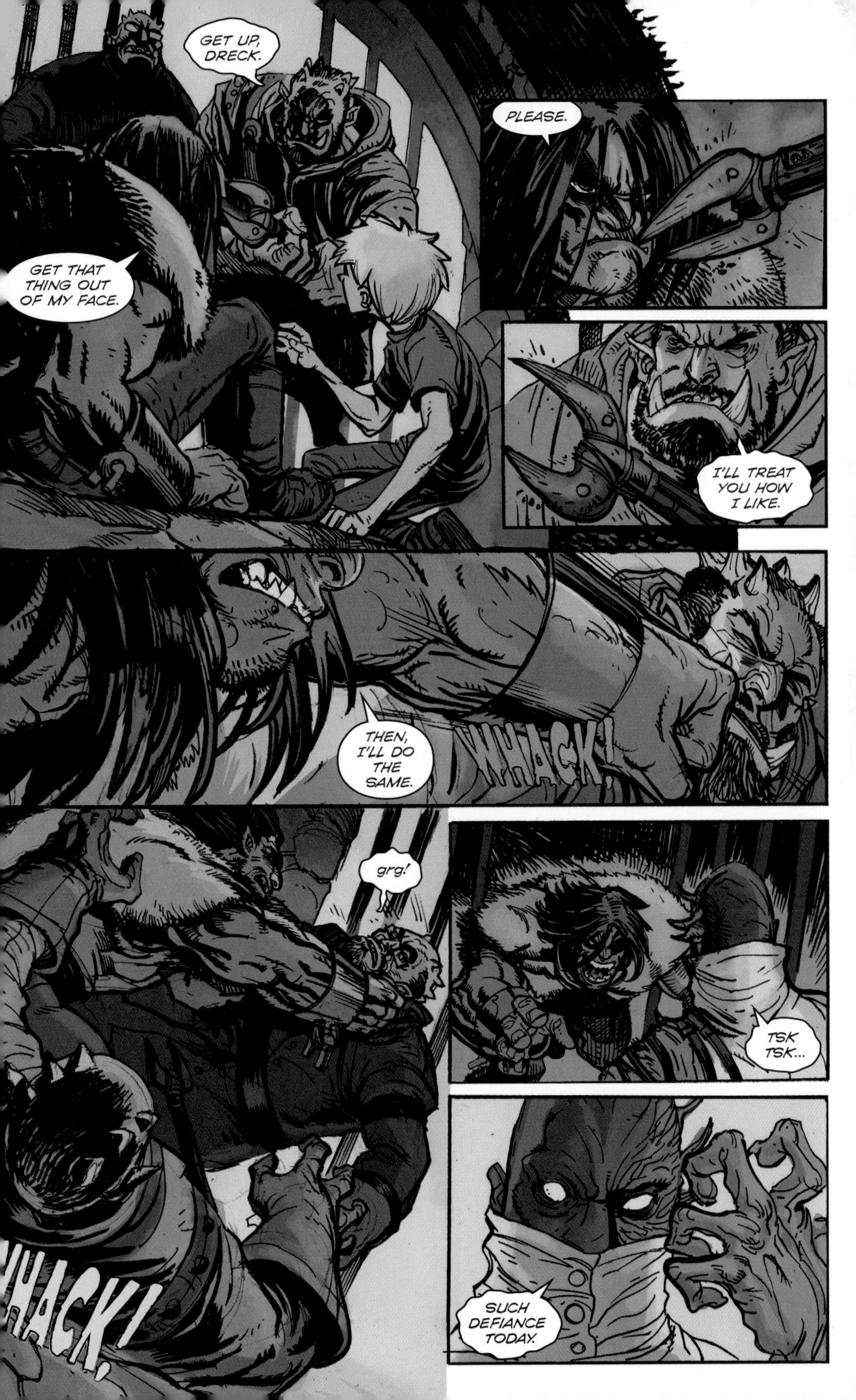
GET UP, DRECK.
GET THAT THING OUT OF MY FACE.
PLEASE.
I'LL TREAT YOU HOW I LIKE.
THEN, I'LL DO THE SAME.
WHACK!
grg!
HACK!
TSK TSK...
SUCH DEFIANCE TODAY.

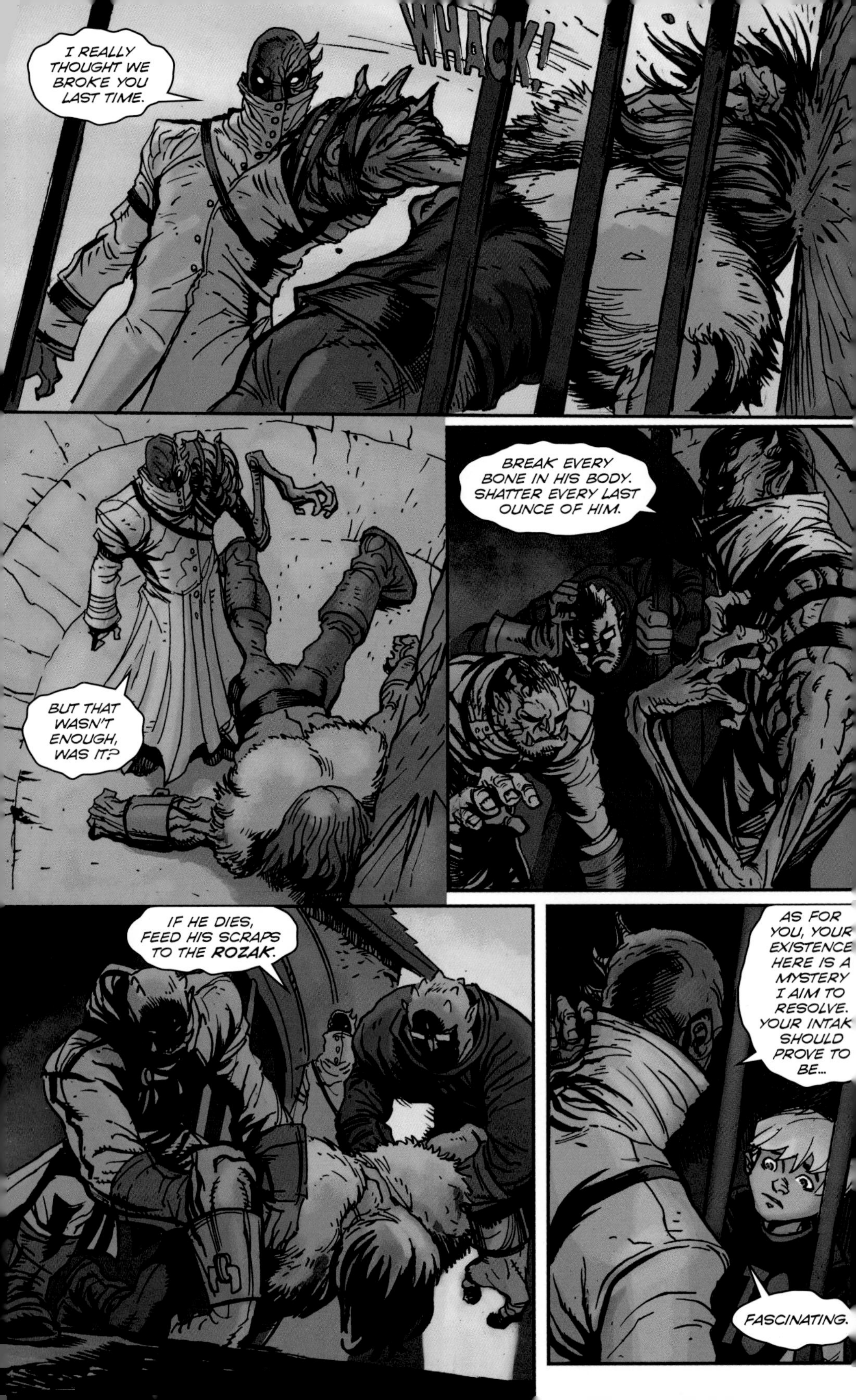
WHACK!
I REALLY THOUGHT WE BROKE YOU LAST TIME.
BUT THAT WASN'T ENOUGH, WAS IT?
BREAK EVERY BONE IN HIS BODY. SHATTER EVERY LAST OUNCE OF HIM.
IF HE DIES, FEED HIS SCRAPS TO THE ROZAK.
AS FOR YOU, YOUR EXISTENCE HERE IS A MYSTERY I AIM TO RESOLVE. YOUR INTAK SHOULD PROVE TO BE...
FASCINATING.

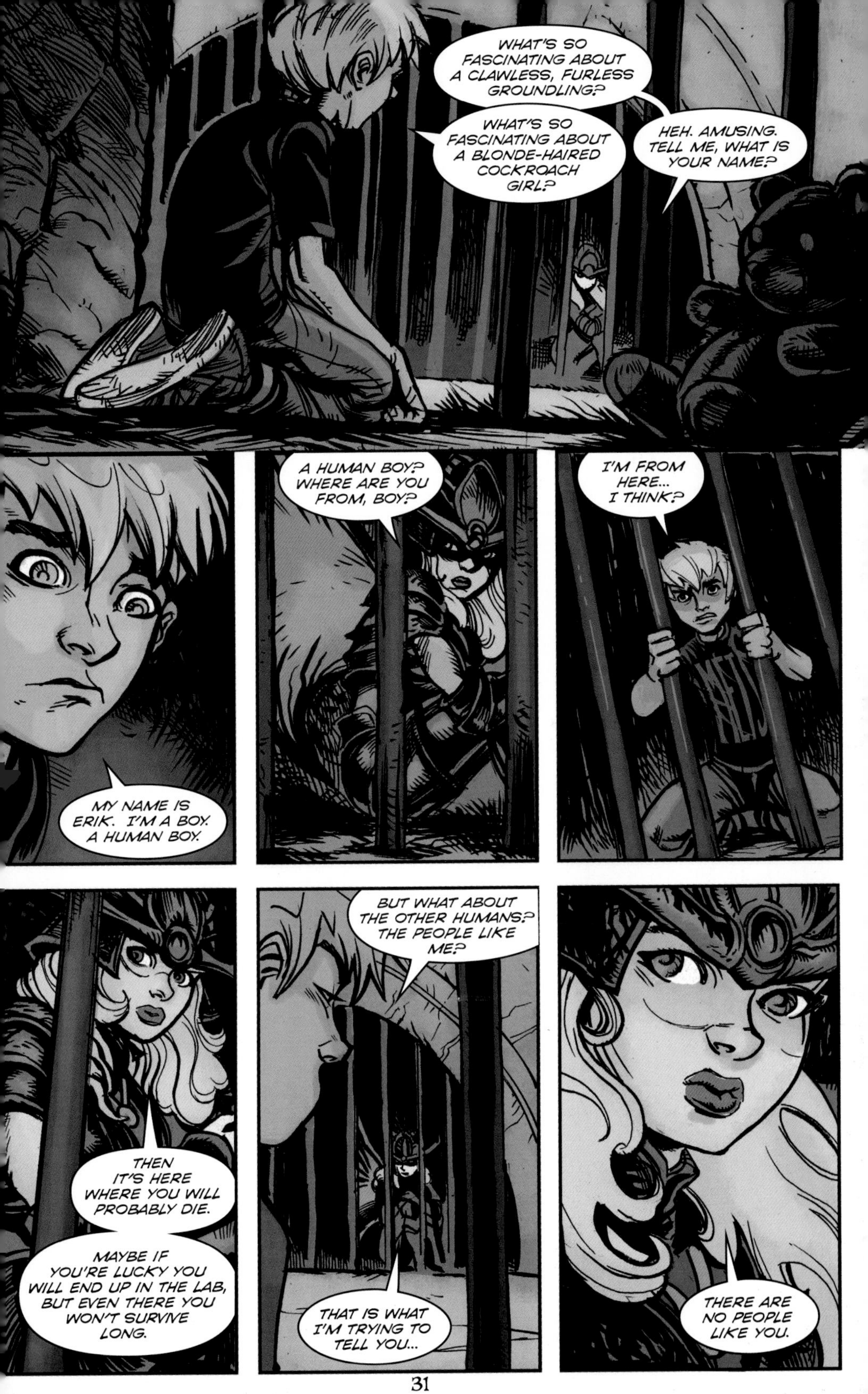
WHAT'S SO FASCINATING ABOUT A BLONDE-HAIRED COCKROACH GIRL?
WHAT'S SO FASCINATING ABOUT A CLAWLESS, FURLESS GROUNDLING?
HEH. AMUSING. TELL ME, WHAT IS YOUR NAME?
MY NAME IS ERIK. I'M A BOY. A HUMAN BOY.
A HUMAN BOY? WHERE ARE YOU FROM, BOY?
I'M FROM HERE... I THINK?
THEN IT'S HERE WHERE YOU WILL PROBABLY DIE.
MAYBE IF YOU'RE LUCKY YOU WILL END UP IN THE LAB, BUT EVEN THERE YOU WON'T SURVIVE LONG.
BUT WHAT ABOUT THE OTHER HUMANS? THE PEOPLE LIKE ME?
THAT IS WHAT I'M TRYING TO TELL YOU...
THERE ARE NO PEOPLE LIKE YOU.

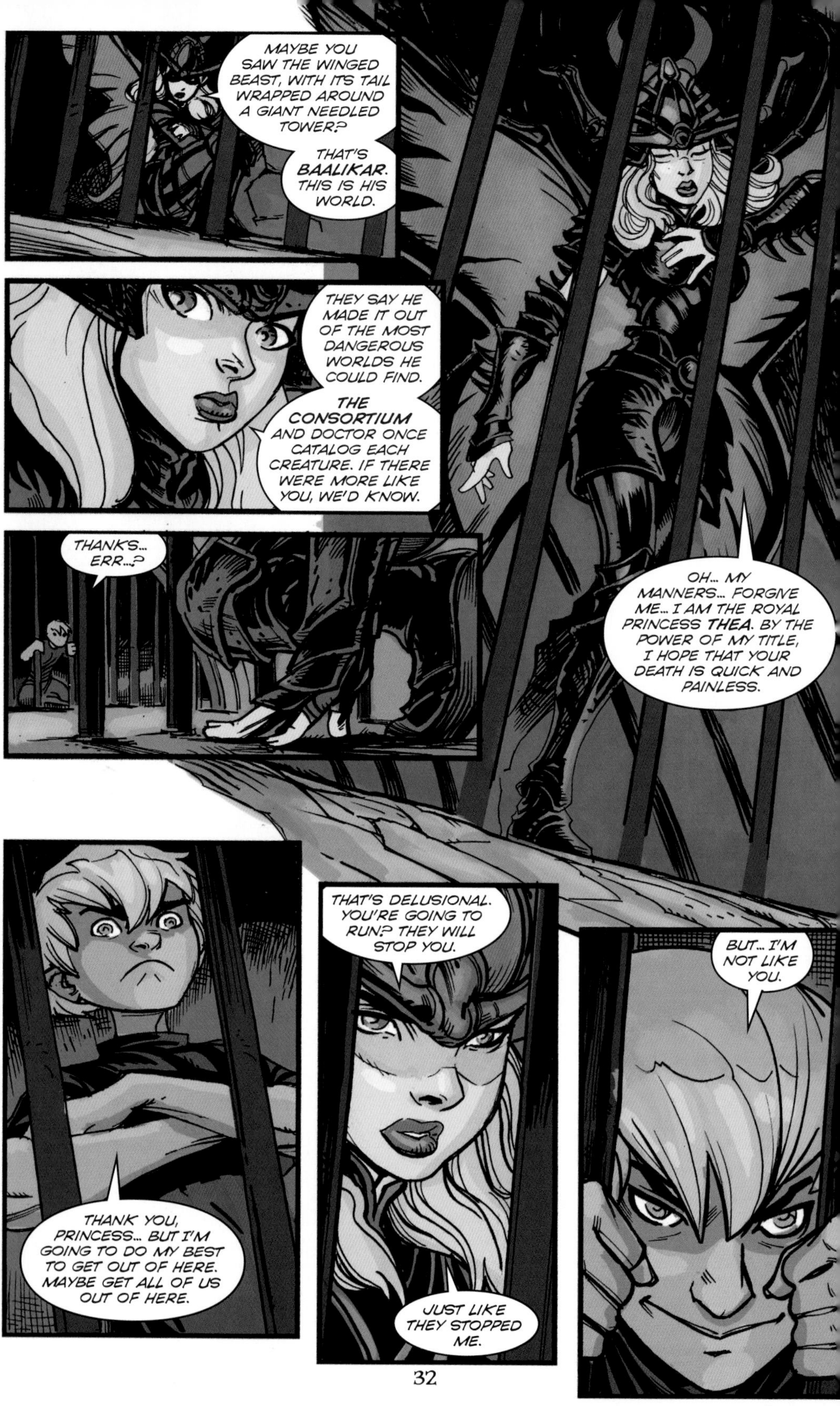
MAYBE YOU SAW THE WINGED BEAST, WITH ITS TAIL WRAPPED AROUND A GIANT NEEDLED TOWER?
THAT'S BAALIKAR. THIS IS HIS WORLD.
THEY SAY HE MADE IT OUT OF THE MOST DANGEROUS WORLDS HE COULD FIND.
THE CONSORTIUM AND DOCTOR ONCE CATALOG EACH CREATURE. IF THERE WERE MORE LIKE YOU, WE'D KNOW.
THANKS... ERR...?
OH... MY MANNERS... FORGIVE ME... I AM THE ROYAL PRINCESS THEA. BY THE POWER OF MY TITLE, I HOPE THAT YOUR DEATH IS QUICK AND PAINLESS.
THANK YOU, PRINCESS... BUT I'M GOING TO DO MY BEST TO GET OUT OF HERE. MAYBE GET ALL OF US OUT OF HERE.
THAT'S DELUSIONAL. YOU'RE GOING TO RUN? THEY WILL STOP YOU.
JUST LIKE THEY STOPPED ME.
BUT... I'M NOT LIKE YOU.

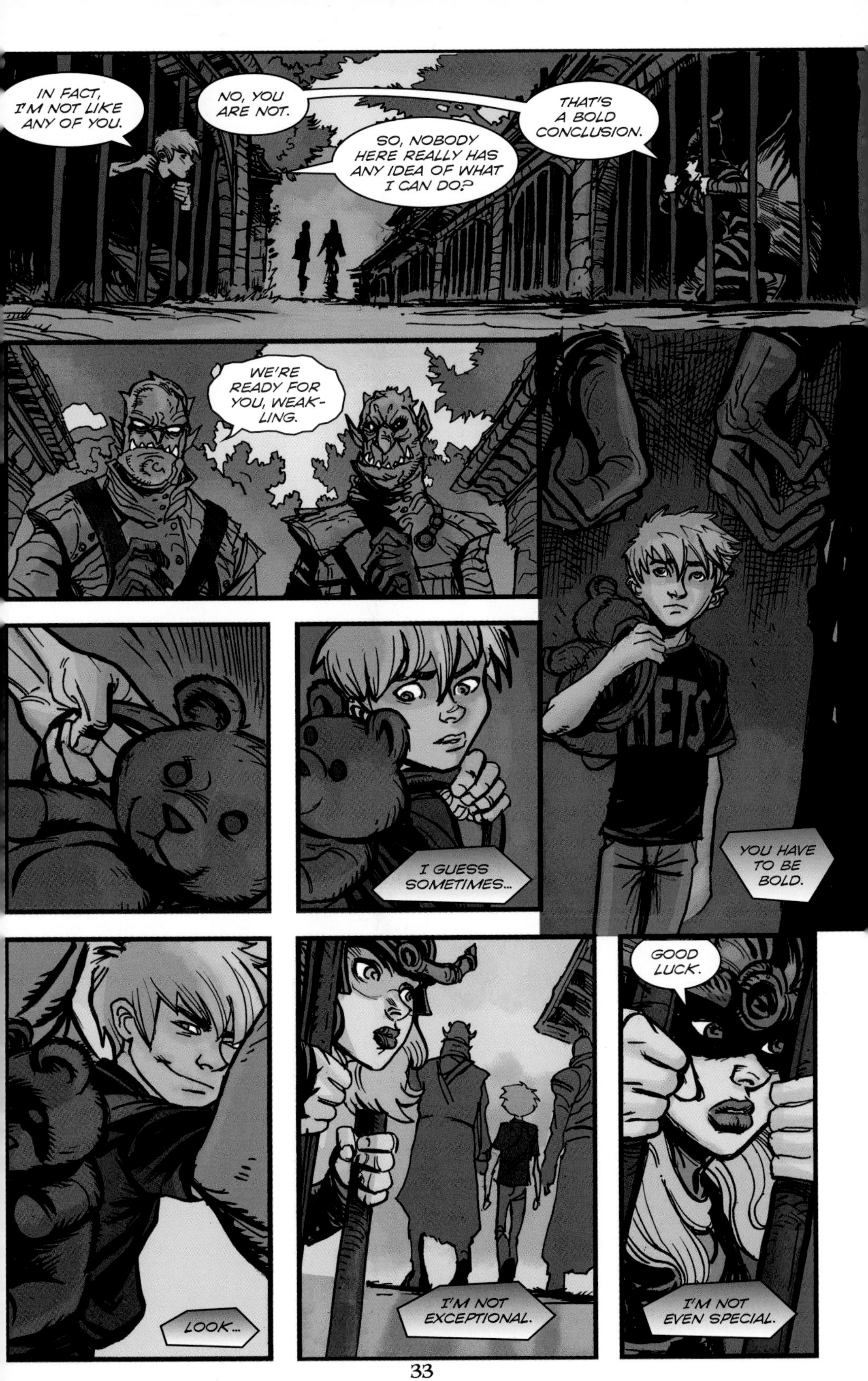
IN FACT, I'M NOT LIKE ANY OF YOU.
NO, YOU ARE NOT.
THAT'S A BOLD CONCLUSION.
SO, NOBODY HERE REALLY HAS ANY IDEA OF WHAT I CAN DO?
WE'RE READY FOR YOU, WEAK-LING.
METS
YOU HAVE TO BE BOLD.
I GUESS SOMETIMES...
LOOK...
I'M NOT EXCEPTIONAL.
GOOD LUCK.
I'M NOT EVEN SPECIAL.

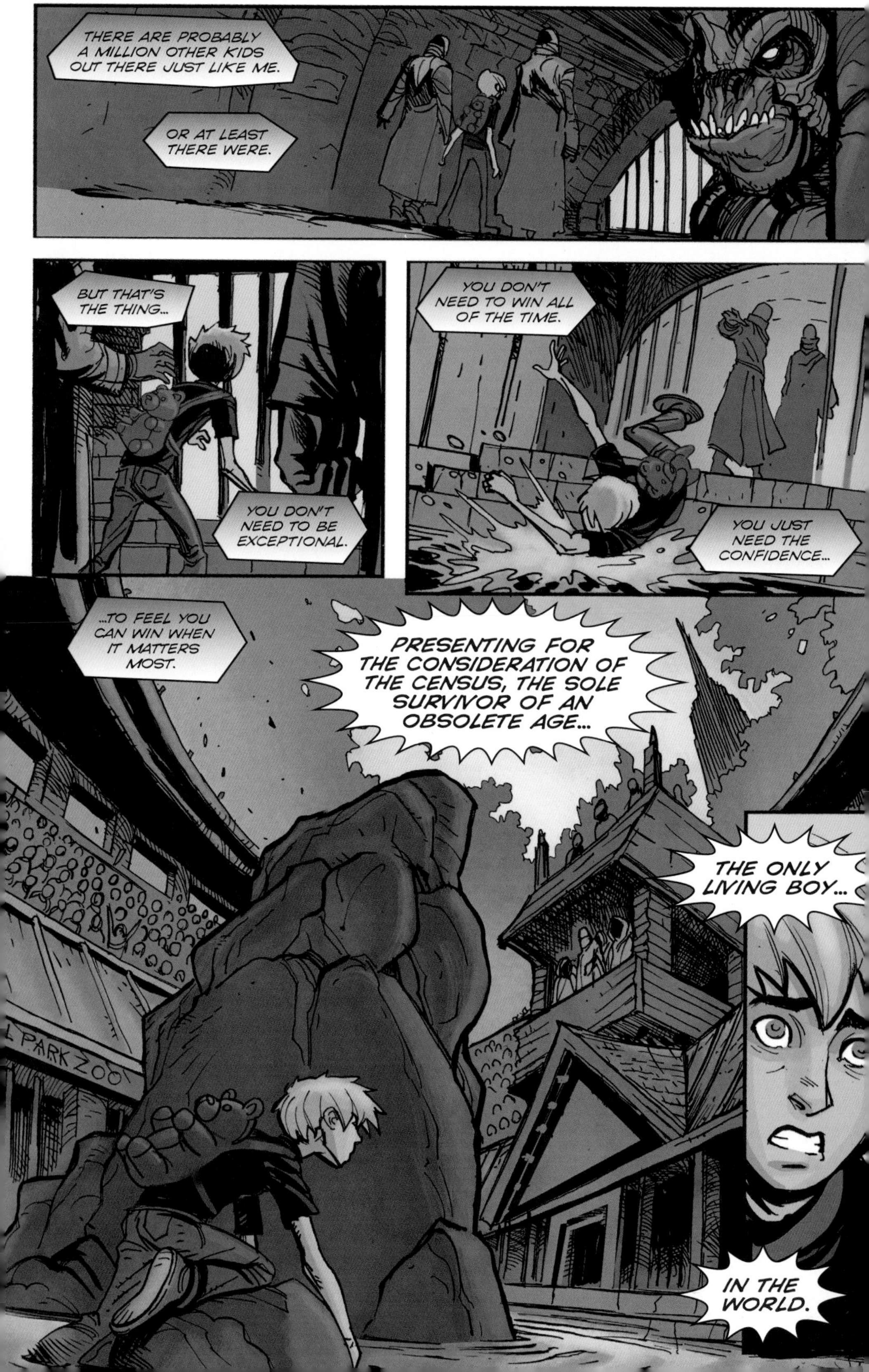
THERE ARE PROBABLY A MILLION OTHER KIDS OUT THERE JUST LIKE ME.
OR AT LEAST THERE WERE.
BUT THAT'S THE THING...
YOU DON'T NEED TO BE EXCEPTIONAL.
YOU DON'T NEED TO WIN ALL OF THE TIME.
YOU JUST NEED THE CONFIDENCE...
...TO FEEL YOU CAN WIN WHEN IT MATTERS MOST.
PRESENTING FOR THE CONSIDERATION OF THE CENSUS, THE SOLE SURVIVOR OF AN OBSOLETE AGE...
PARK ZOO
THE ONLY LIVING BOY...
IN THE WORLD.

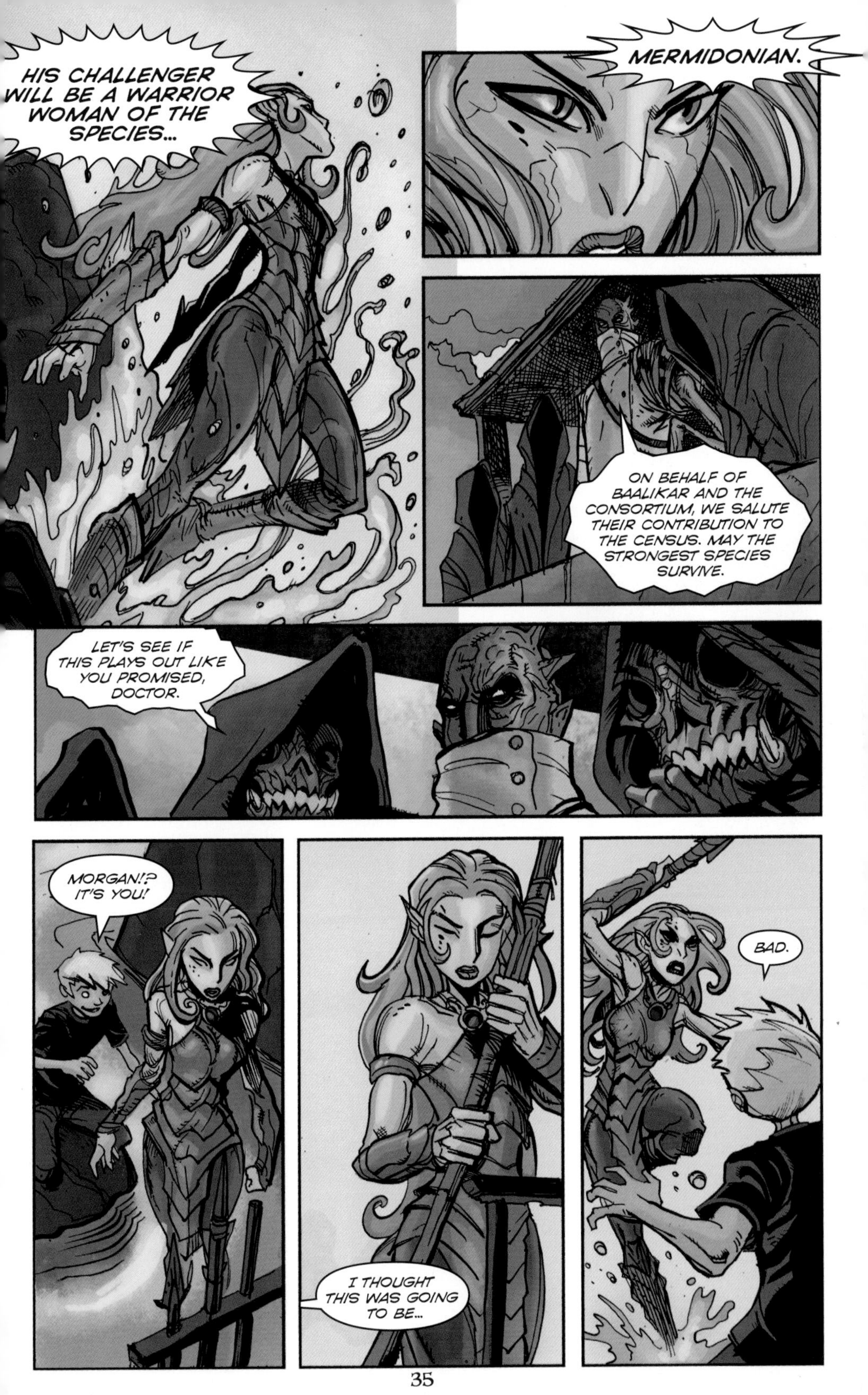
HIS CHALLENGER WILL BE A WARRIOR WOMAN OF THE SPECIES...
MERMIDONIAN.
ON BEHALF OF BAALIKAR AND THE CONSORTIUM, WE SALUTE THEIR CONTRIBUTION TO THE CENSUS. MAY THE STRONGEST SPECIES SURVIVE.
LET'S SEE IF THIS PLAYS OUT LIKE YOU PROMISED, DOCTOR.
MORGAN!? IT'S YOU!
I THOUGHT THIS WAS GOING TO BE...
BAD.

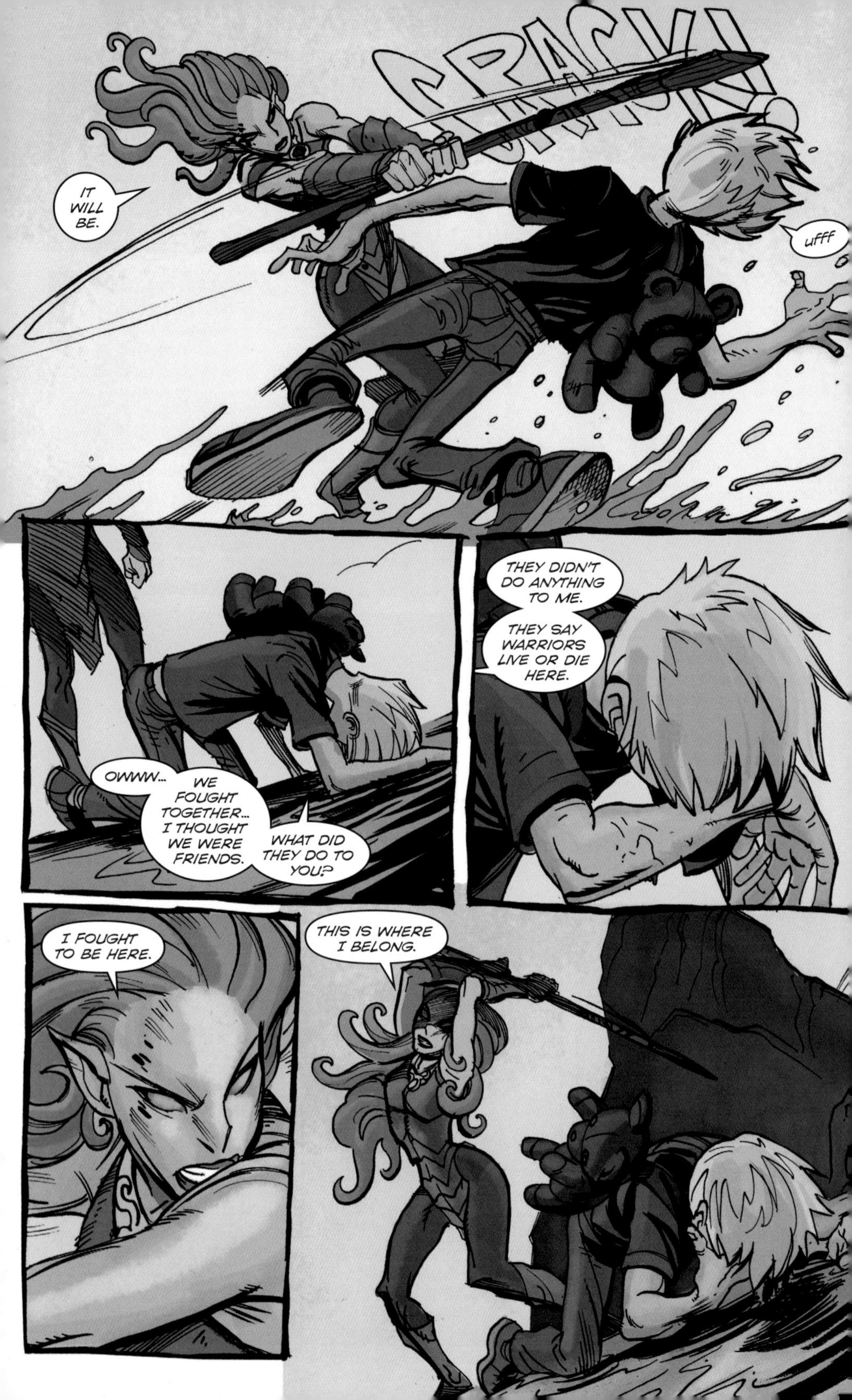
CRACK!
IT WILL BE.
ufff
OWWW...
WE FOUGHT TOGETHER... I THOUGHT WE WERE FRIENDS.
WHAT DID THEY DO TO YOU?
THEY DIDN'T DO ANYTHING TO ME.
THEY SAY WARRIORS LIVE OR DIE HERE.
I FOUGHT TO BE HERE.
THIS IS WHERE I BELONG.

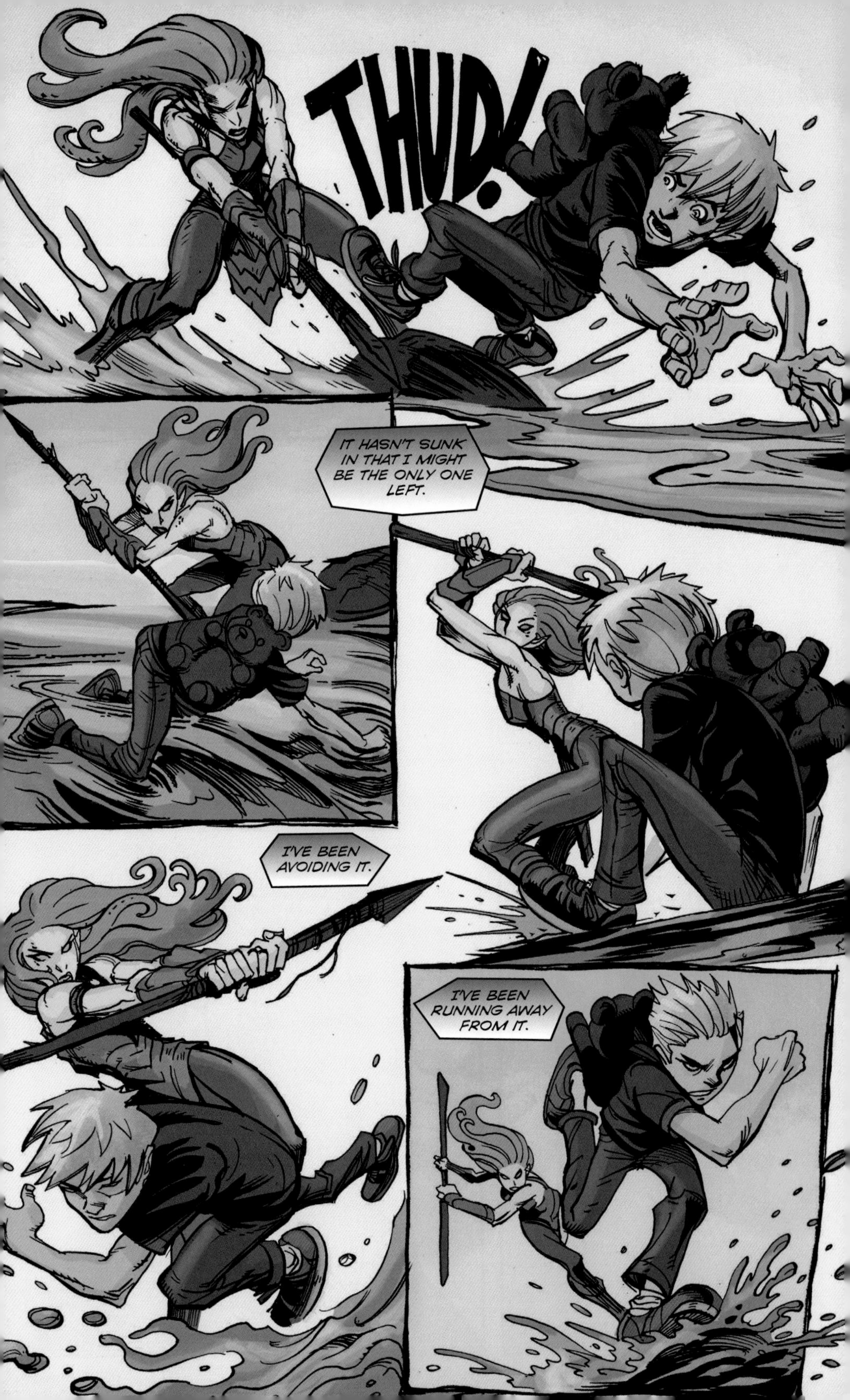
THUD!
IT HASN'T SUNK IN THAT I MIGHT BE THE ONLY ONE LEFT.
I'VE BEEN AVOIDING IT.
I'VE BEEN RUNNING AWAY FROM IT.

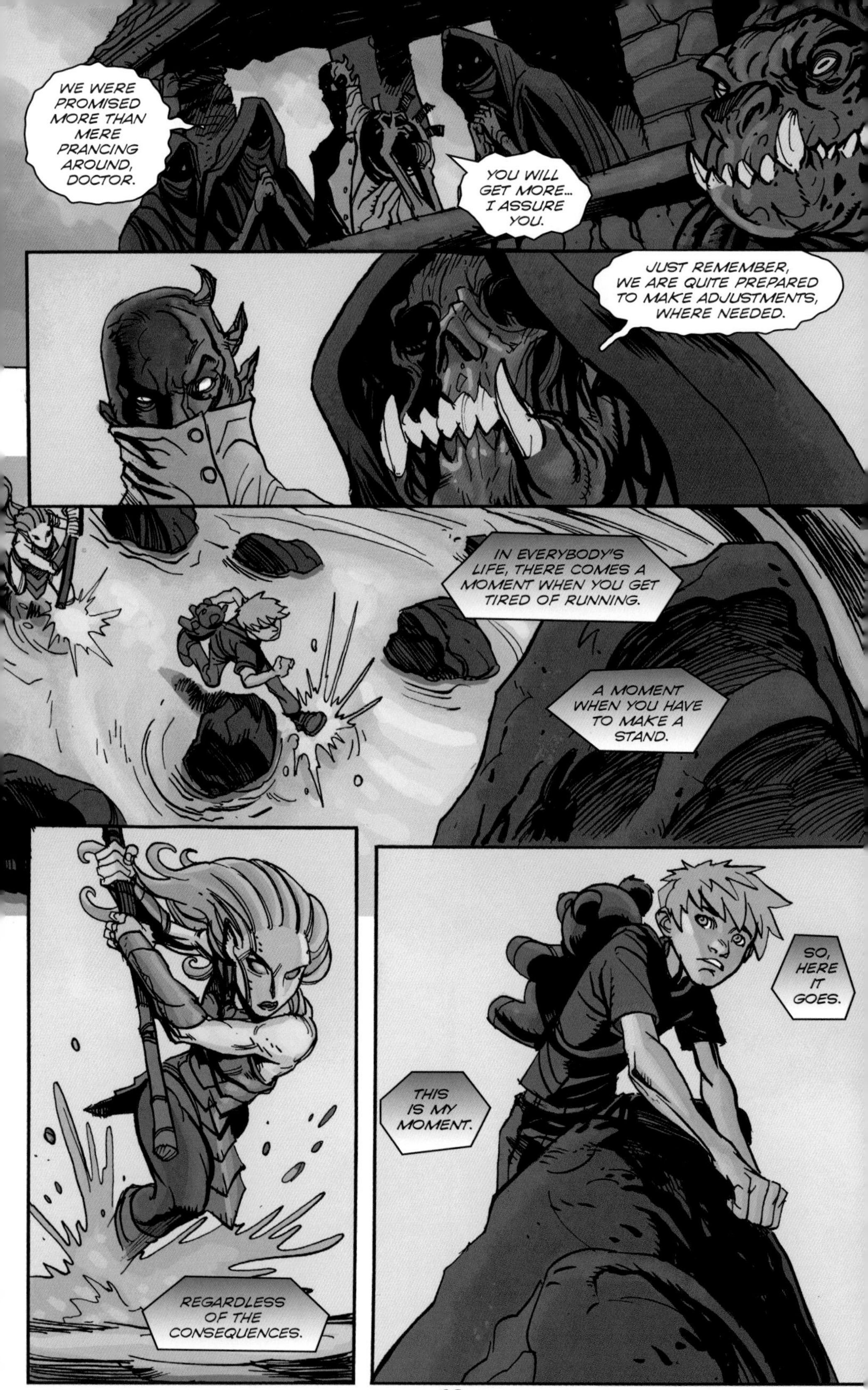
WE WERE PROMISED MORE THAN MERE PRANCING AROUND, DOCTOR.
YOU WILL GET MORE... I ASSURE YOU.
JUST REMEMBER, WE ARE QUITE PREPARED TO MAKE ADJUSTMENTS, WHERE NEEDED.
IN EVERYBODY'S LIFE, THERE COMES A MOMENT WHEN YOU GET TIRED OF RUNNING.
A MOMENT WHEN YOU HAVE TO MAKE A STAND.
REGARDLESS OF THE CONSEQUENCES.
SO, HERE IT GOES.
THIS IS MY MOMENT.

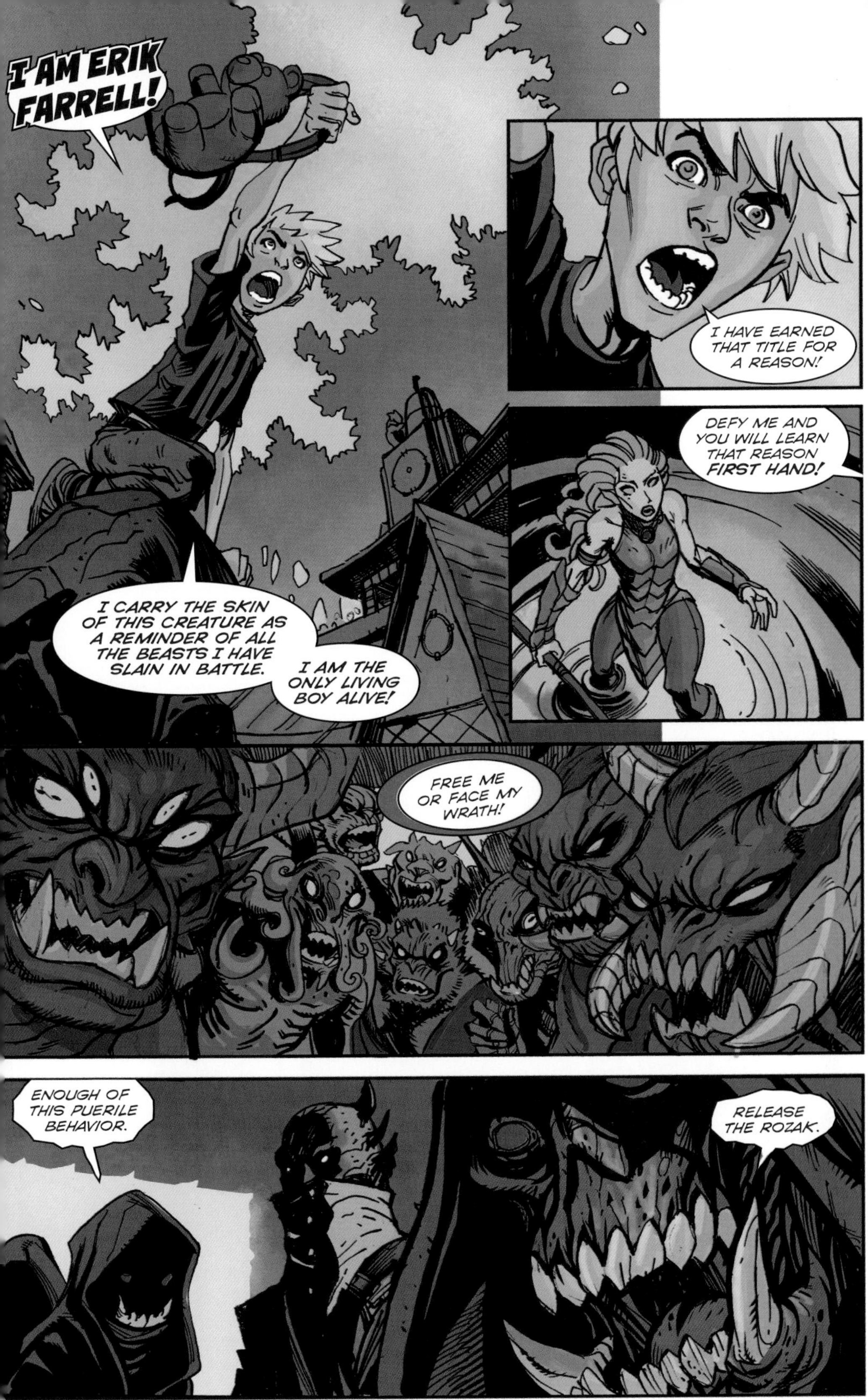
I AM ERIK FARRELL!
I HAVE EARNED THAT TITLE FOR A REASON!
DEFY ME AND YOU WILL LEARN THAT REASON FIRST HAND!
I CARRY THE SKIN OF THIS CREATURE AS A REMINDER OF ALL THE BEASTS I HAVE SLAIN IN BATTLE.
I AM THE ONLY LIVING BOY ALIVE!
FREE ME OR FACE MY WRATH!
ENOUGH OF THIS PUERILE BEHAVIOR.
RELEASE THE ROZAK.

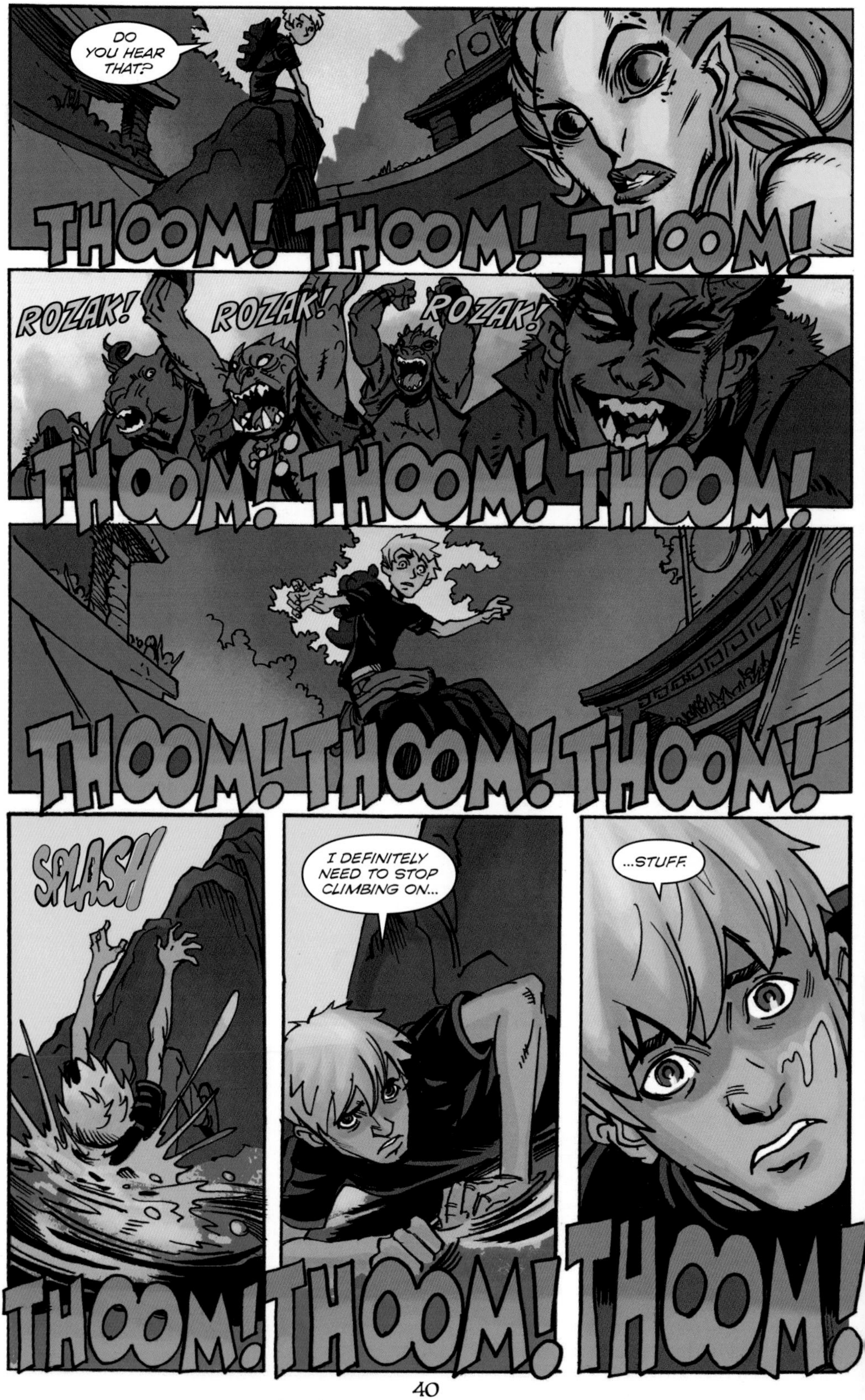
DO YOU HEAR THAT?
THOOM! THOOM! THOOM!
ROZAK! ROZAK! ROZAK!
THOOM! THOOM! THOOM!
THOOM! THOOM! THOOM!
SPLASH
I DEFINITELY NEED TO STOP CLIMBING ON...
...STUFF.
THOOM! THOOM! THOOM!

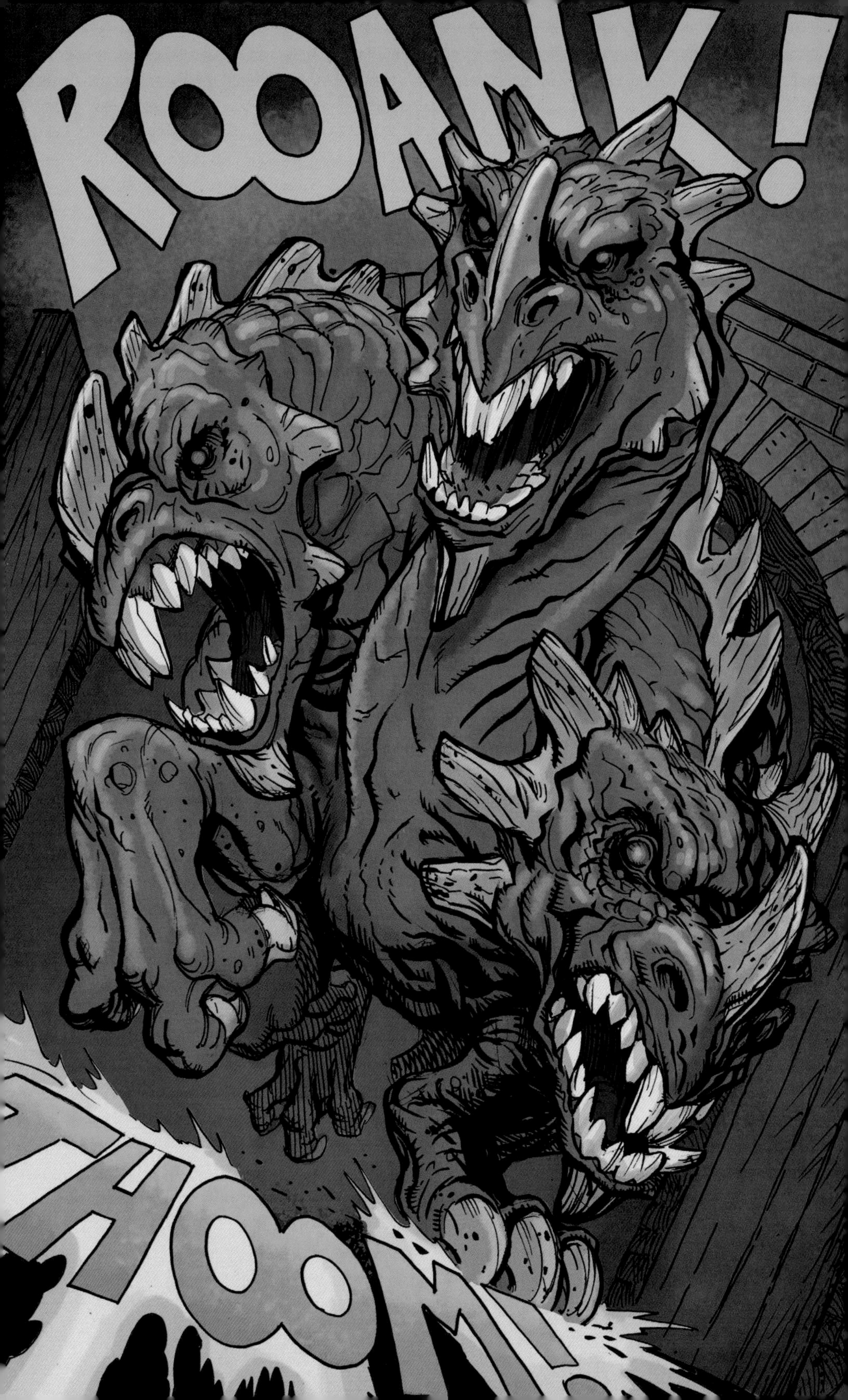
ROOANK!
HOOM

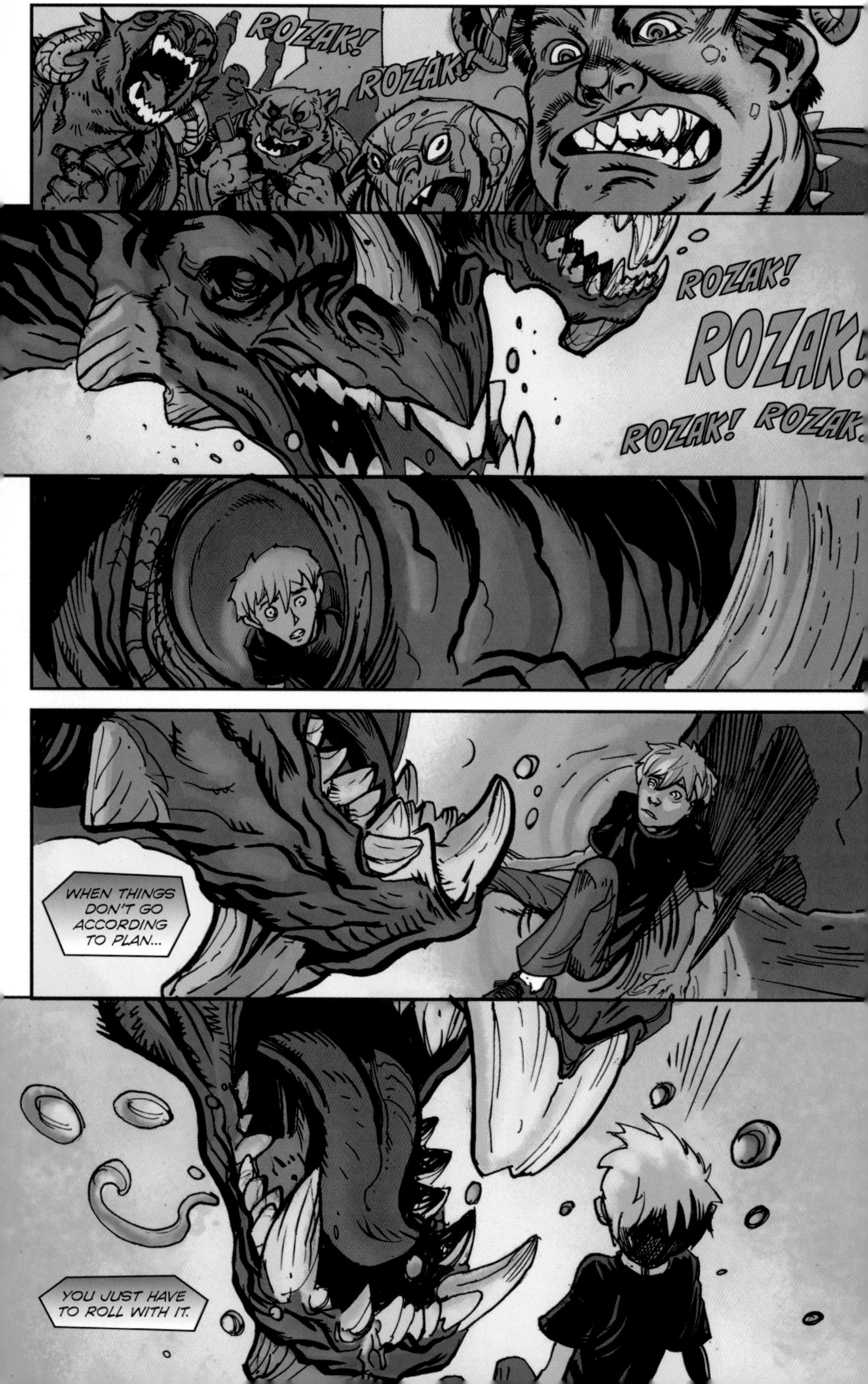
ROZAK!
ROZAK!
ROZAK!
ROZAK!
ROZAK! ROZAK!
WHEN THINGS DON'T GO ACCORDING TO PLAN...
YOU JUST HAVE TO ROLL WITH IT.

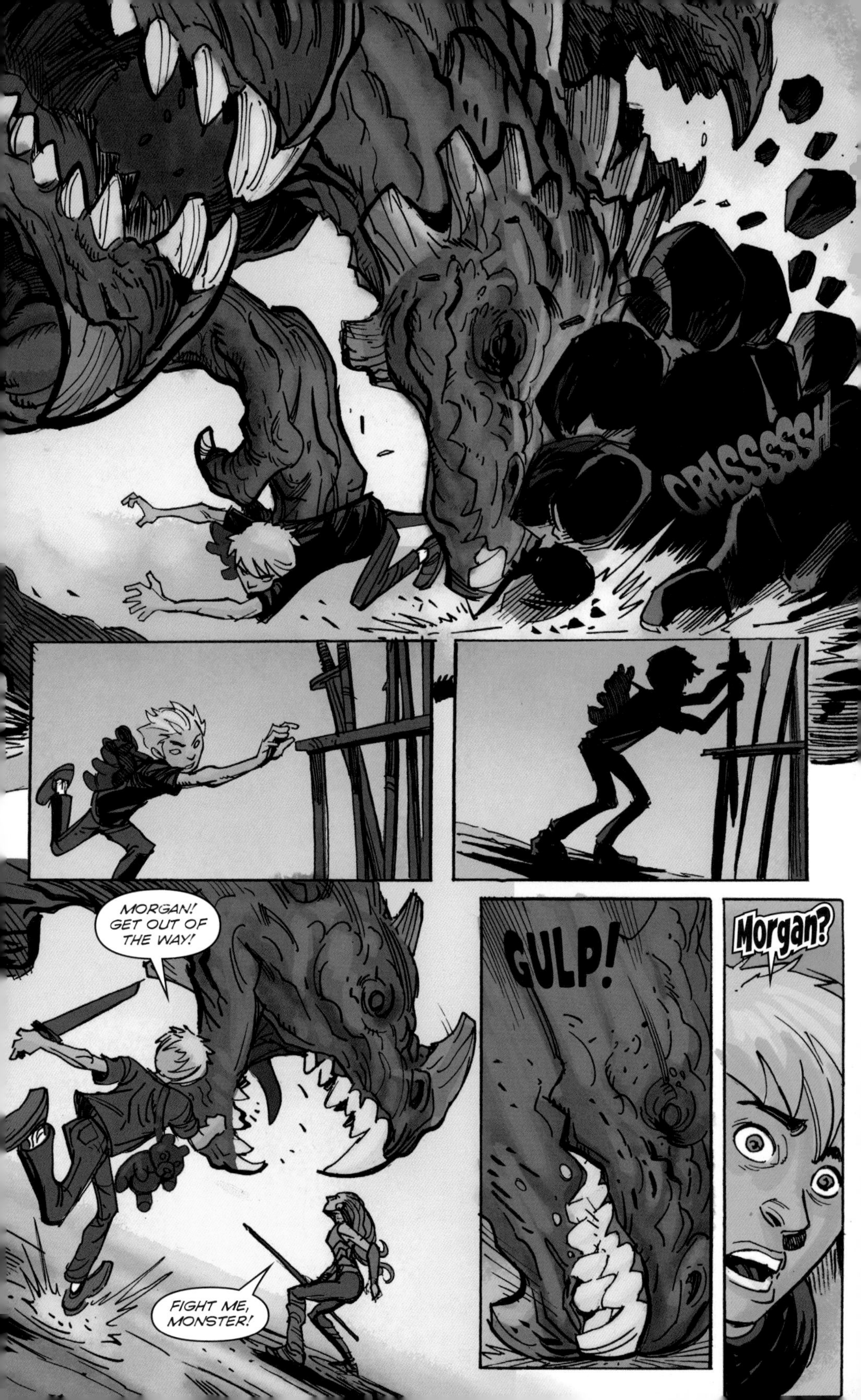
CRASSSSSH
MORGAN! GET OUT OF THE WAY!
FIGHT ME, MONSTER!
GULP!
Morgan?

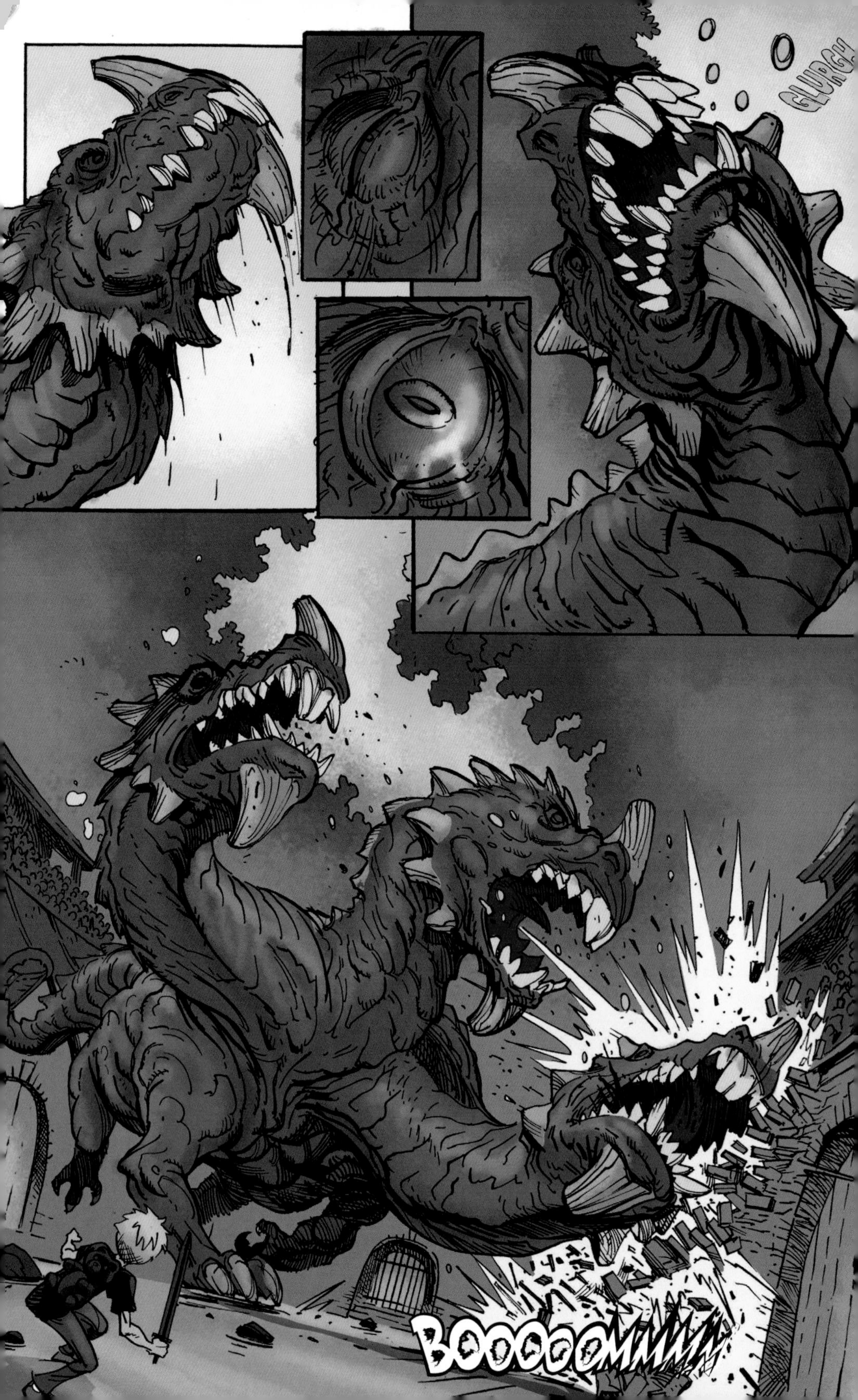
GLURGH
BOOOOOMMMMM

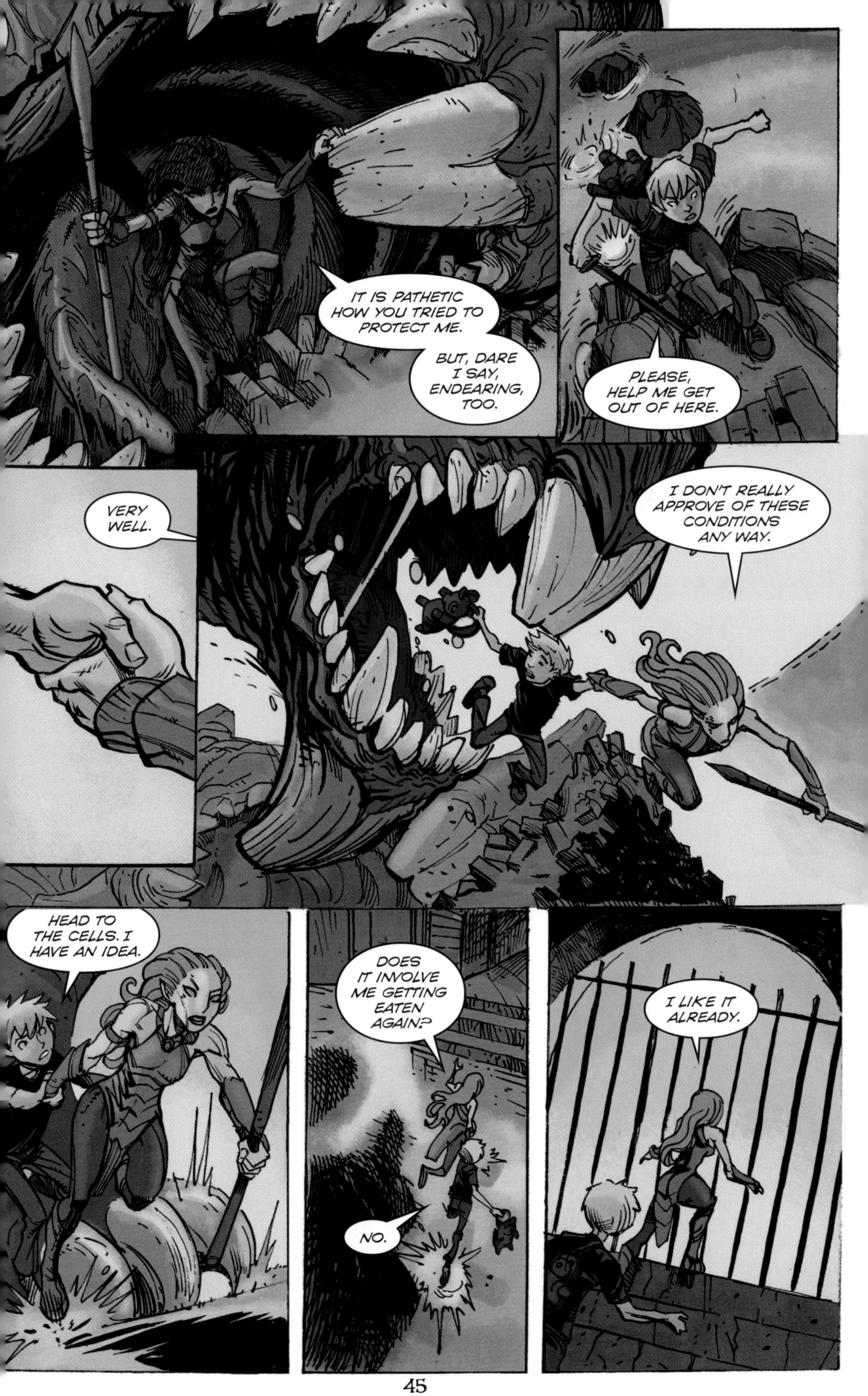
IT IS PATHETIC HOW YOU TRIED TO PROTECT ME.
BUT, DARE I SAY, ENDEARING, TOO.
PLEASE, HELP ME GET OUT OF HERE.
VERY WELL.
I DON'T REALLY APPROVE OF THESE CONDITIONS ANY WAY.
HEAD TO THE CELLS. I HAVE AN IDEA.
DOES IT INVOLVE ME GETTING EATEN AGAIN?
NO.
I LIKE IT ALREADY.

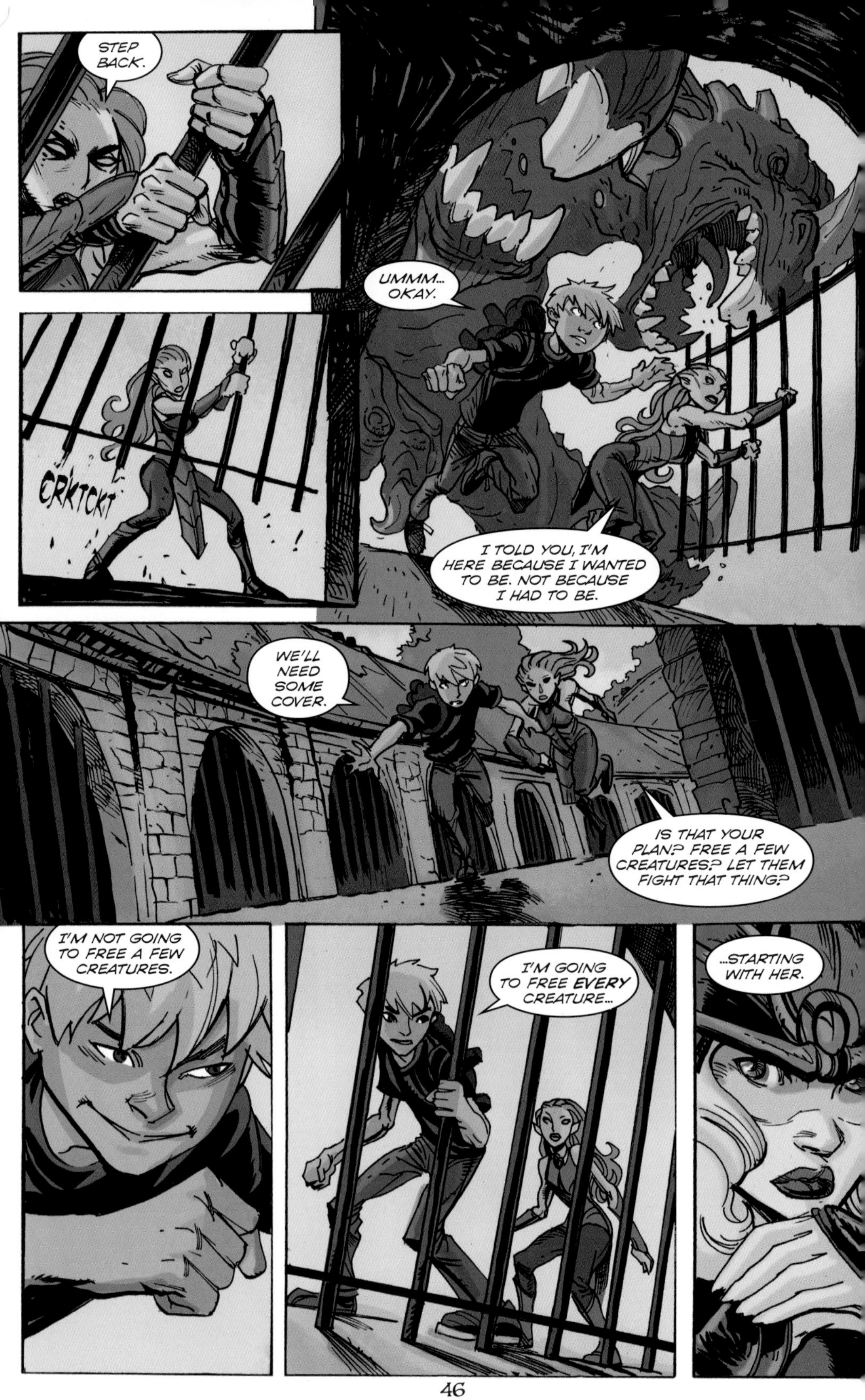
STEP BACK.
UMMM... OKAY.
CRKTCKT
I TOLD YOU, I'M HERE BECAUSE I WANTED TO BE. NOT BECAUSE I HAD TO BE.
WE'LL NEED SOME COVER.
IS THAT YOUR PLAN? FREE A FEW CREATURES? LET THEM FIGHT THAT THING?
I'M NOT GOING TO FREE A FEW CREATURES.
I'M GOING TO FREE **EVERY** CREATURE...
...STARTING WITH HER.

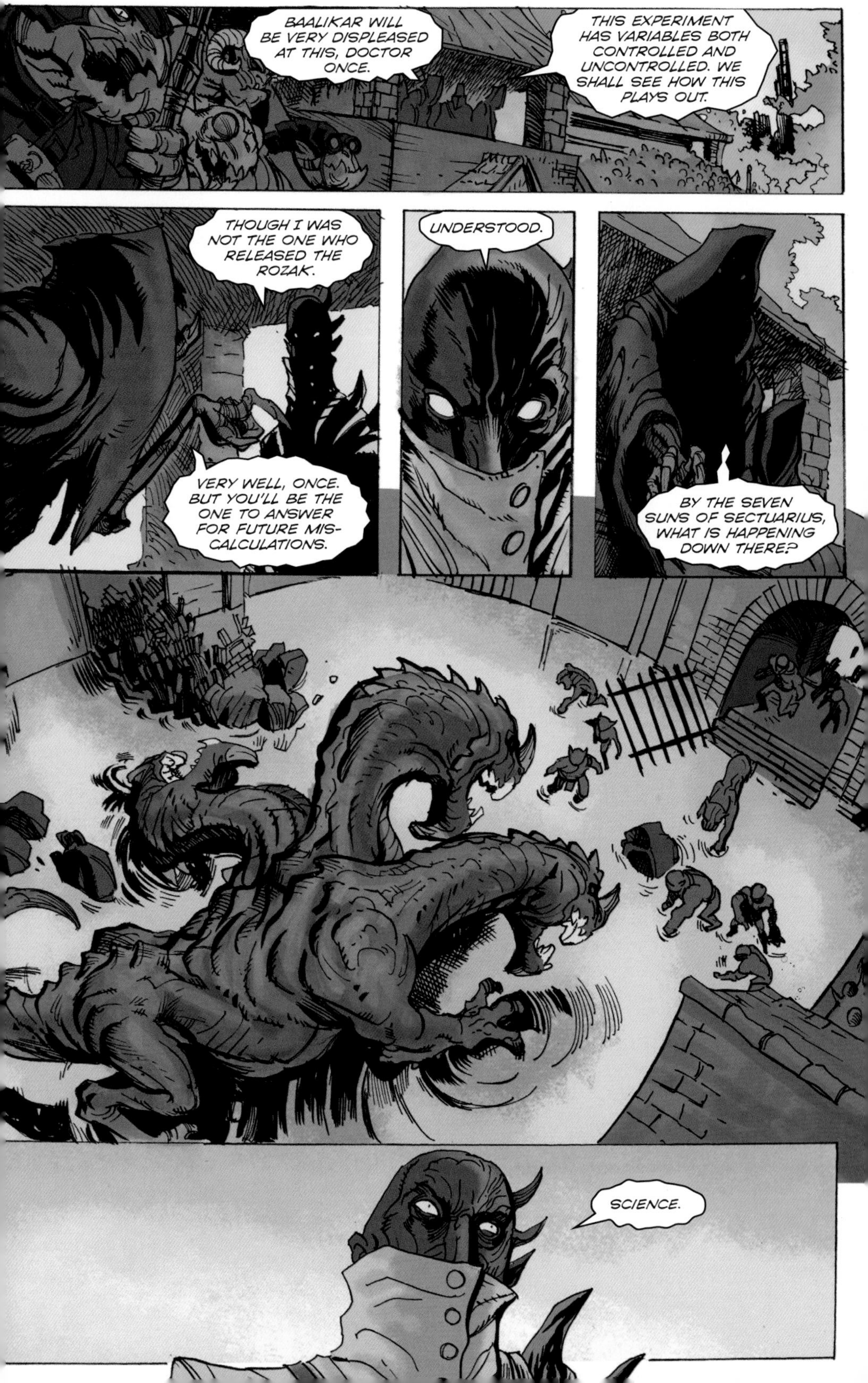
BAALIKAR WILL BE VERY DISPLEASED AT THIS, DOCTOR ONCE.
THIS EXPERIMENT HAS VARIABLES BOTH CONTROLLED AND UNCONTROLLED. WE SHALL SEE HOW THIS PLAYS OUT.
THOUGH I WAS NOT THE ONE WHO RELEASED THE ROZAK.
VERY WELL, ONCE. BUT YOU'LL BE THE ONE TO ANSWER FOR FUTURE MIS-CALCULATIONS.
UNDERSTOOD.
BY THE SEVEN SUNS OF SECTUARIUS, WHAT IS HAPPENING DOWN THERE?
SCIENCE.

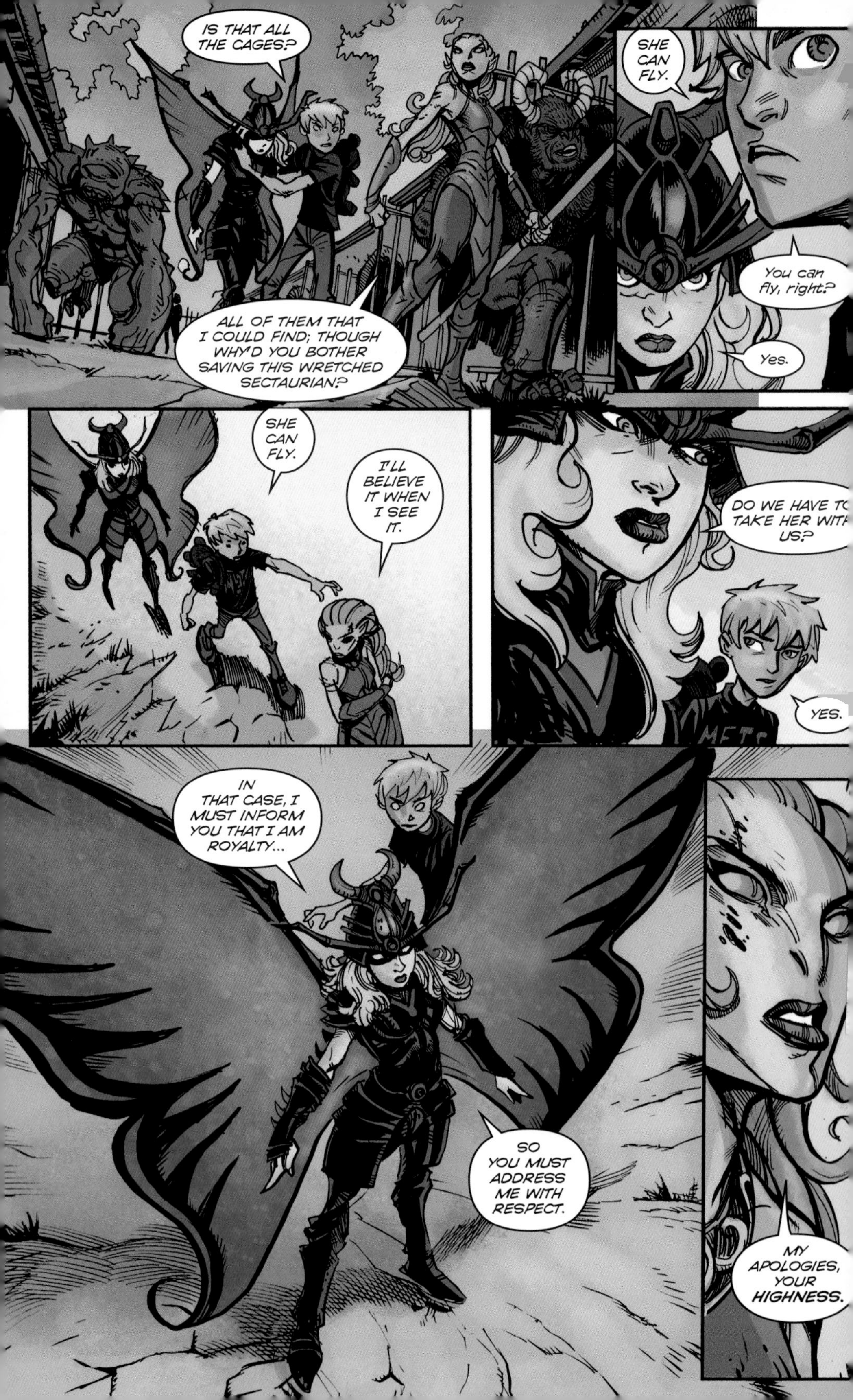
IS THAT ALL THE CAGES?
ALL OF THEM THAT I COULD FIND; THOUGH WHY'D YOU BOTHER SAVING THIS WRETCHED SECTAURIAN?
SHE CAN FLY.
You can fly, right?
Yes.
SHE CAN FLY.
I'LL BELIEVE IT WHEN I SEE IT.
DO WE HAVE TO TAKE HER WITH US?
YES.
IN THAT CASE, I MUST INFORM YOU THAT I AM ROYALTY...
SO YOU MUST ADDRESS ME WITH RESPECT.
MY APOLOGIES, YOUR HIGHNESS.

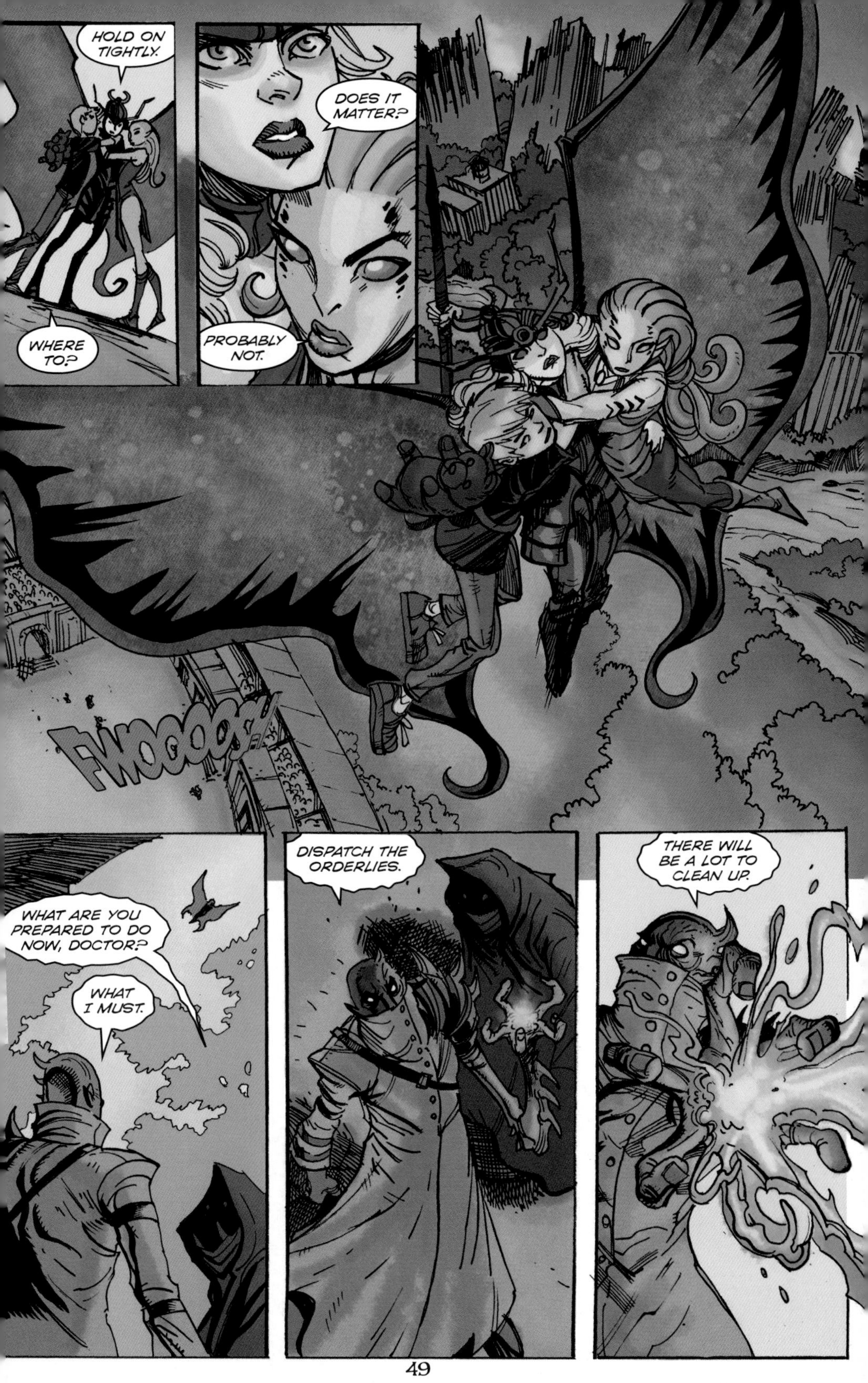
HOLD ON TIGHTLY.
WHERE TO?
DOES IT MATTER?
PROBABLY NOT.
FWOOOSH
WHAT ARE YOU PREPARED TO DO NOW, DOCTOR?
WHAT I MUST.
DISPATCH THE ORDERLIES.
THERE WILL BE A LOT TO CLEAN UP.

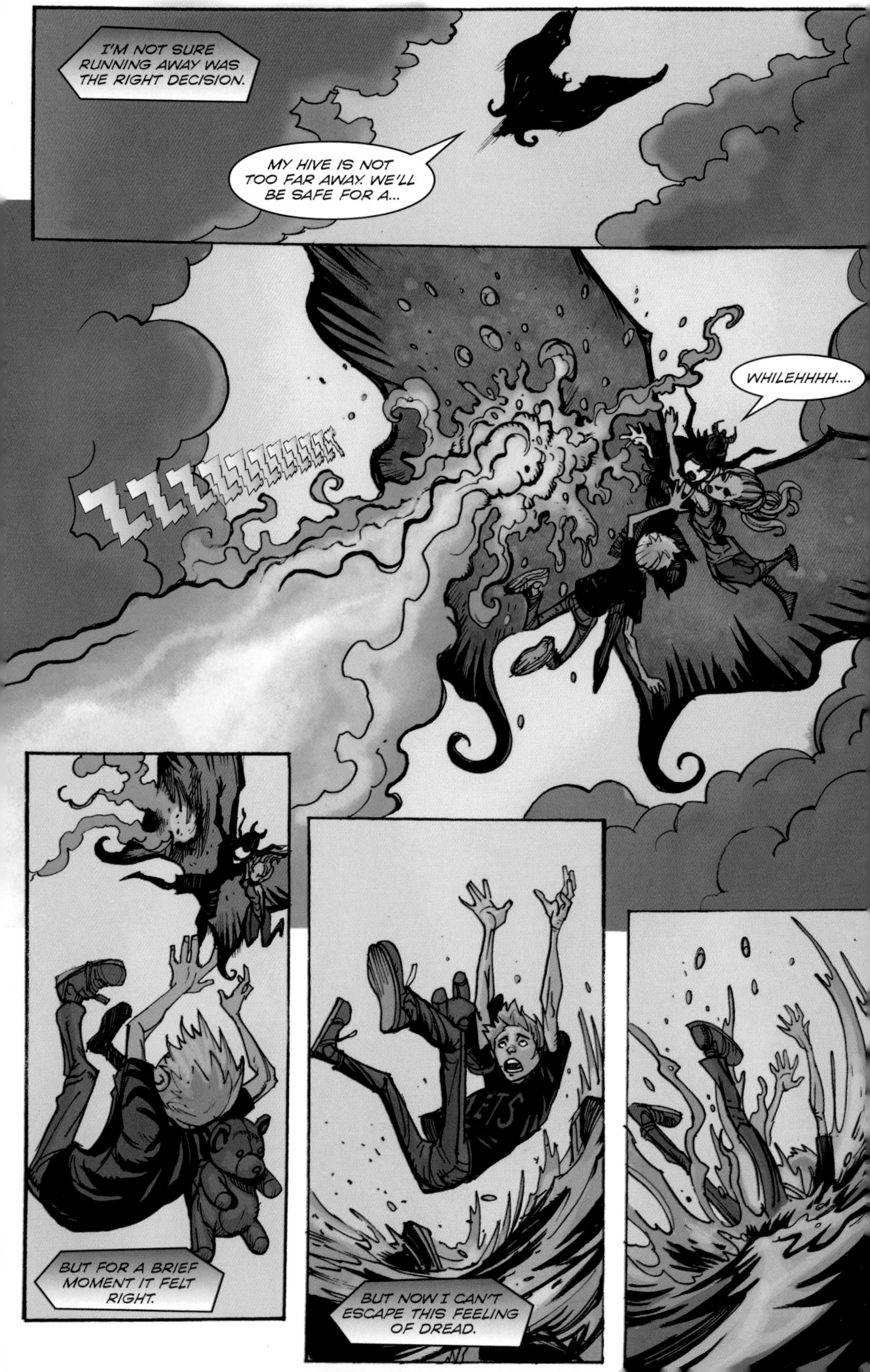
I'M NOT SURE RUNNING AWAY WAS THE RIGHT DECISION.
MY HIVE IS NOT TOO FAR AWAY. WE'LL BE SAFE FOR A...
ZZZZZZZZZZZZZZT
WHILEHHHH....
BUT FOR A BRIEF MOMENT IT FELT RIGHT.
BUT NOW I CAN'T ESCAPE THIS FEELING OF DREAD.

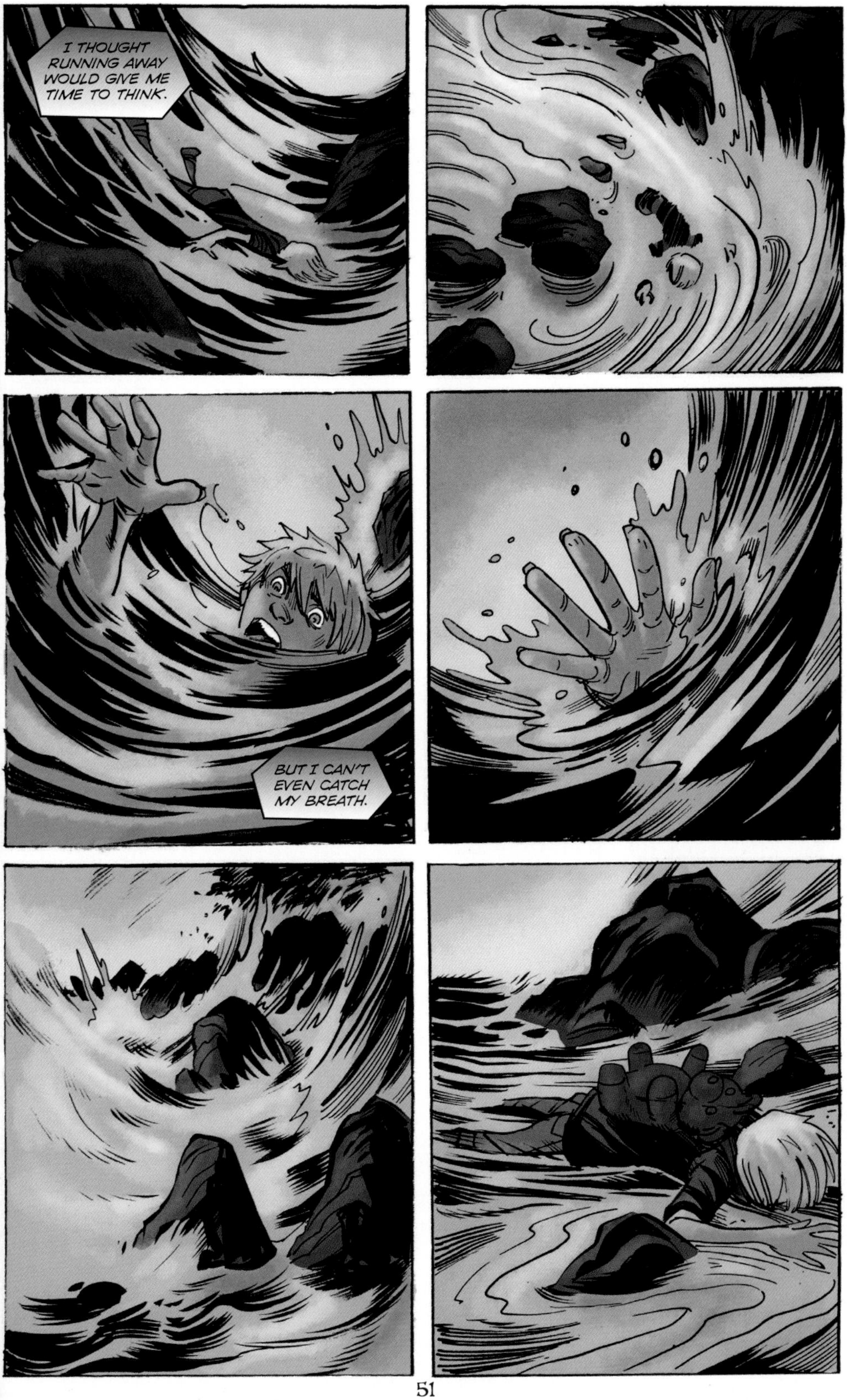
I THOUGHT RUNNING AWAY WOULD GIVE ME TIME TO THINK.
BUT I CAN'T EVEN CATCH MY BREATH.

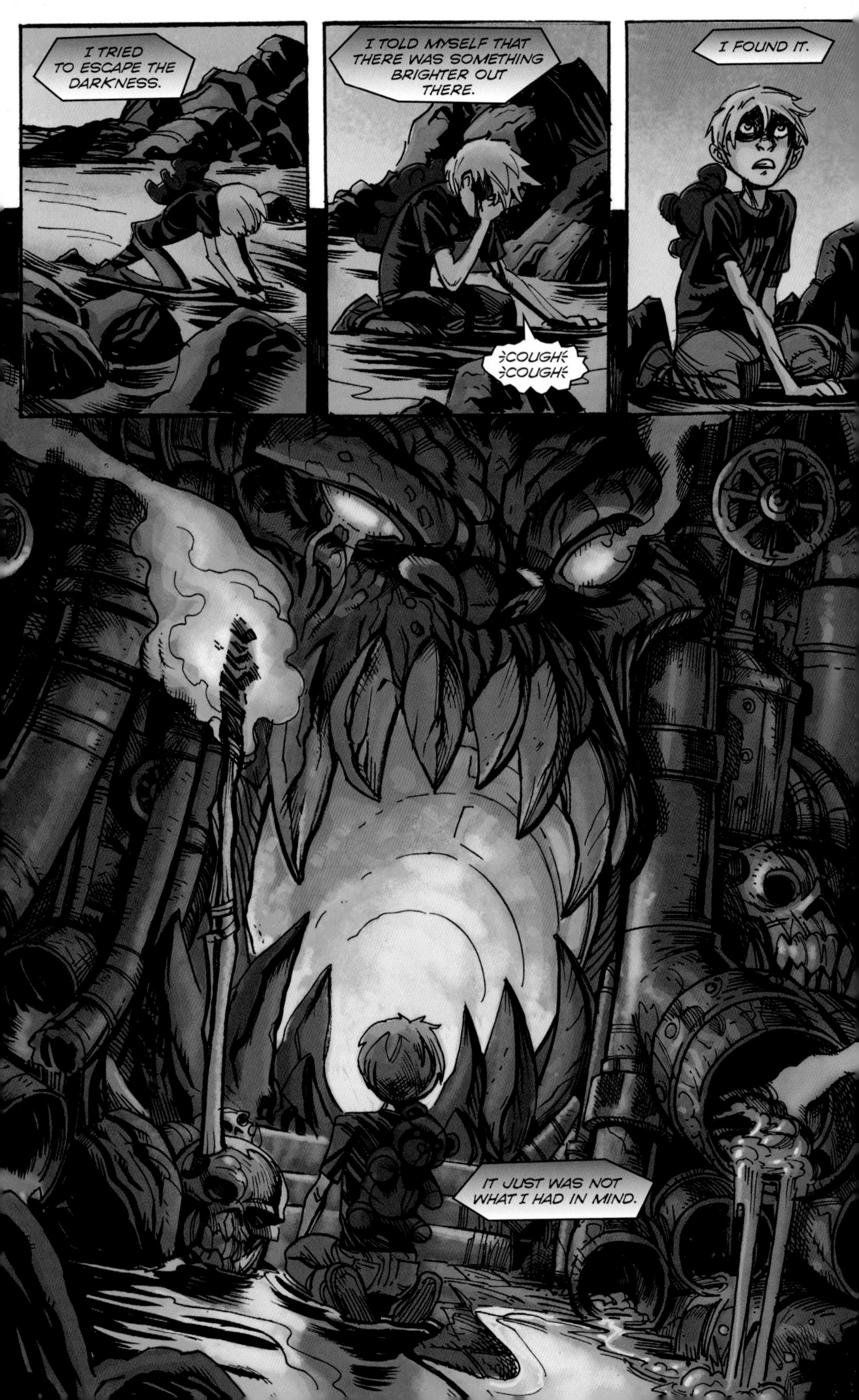
I TRIED TO ESCAPE THE DARKNESS.
I TOLD MYSELF THAT THERE WAS SOMETHING BRIGHTER OUT THERE.
COUGH COUGH
I FOUND IT.
IT JUST WAS NOT WHAT I HAD IN MIND.

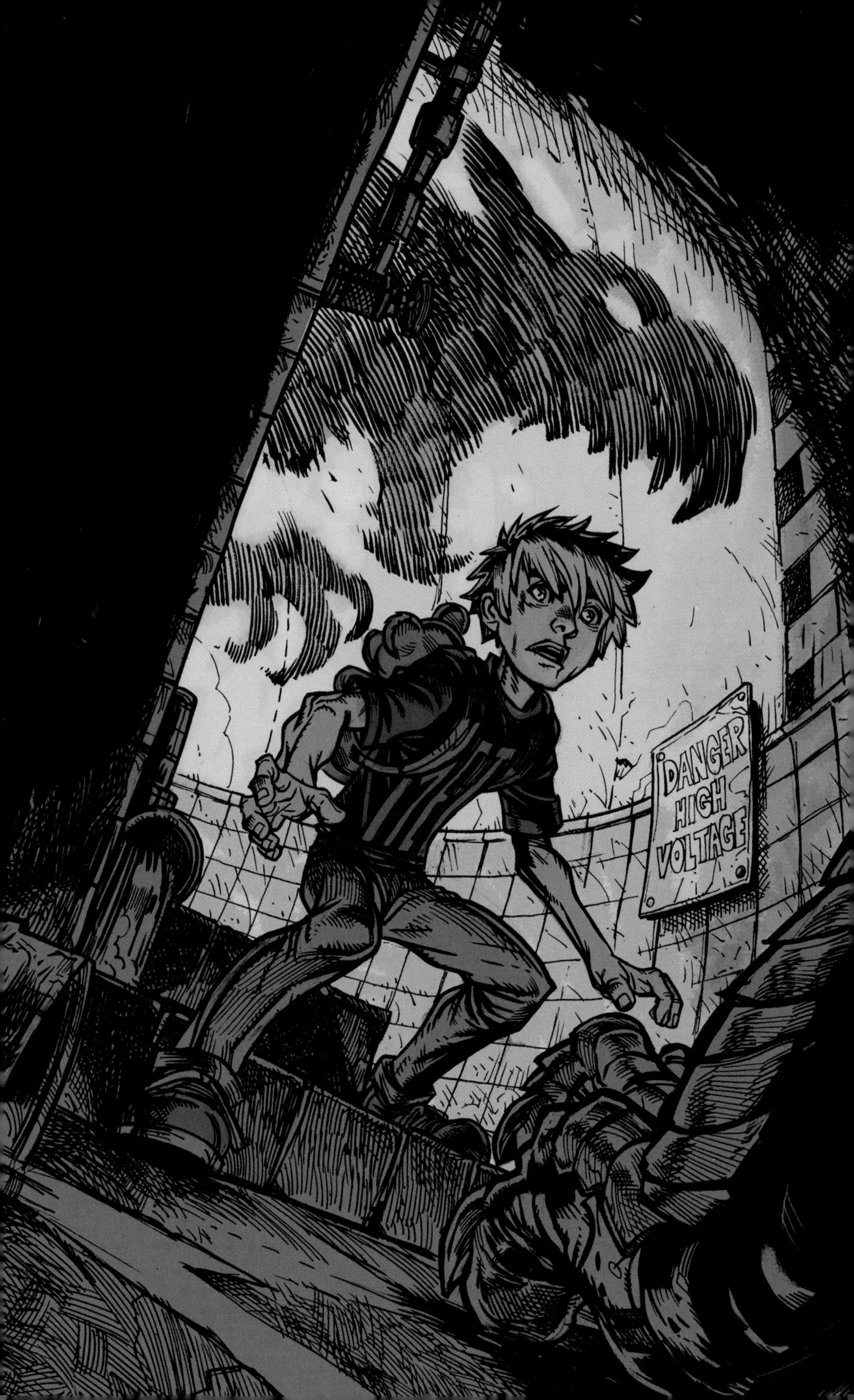
DANGER
HIGH
VOLTAGE

CHAPTER TWO

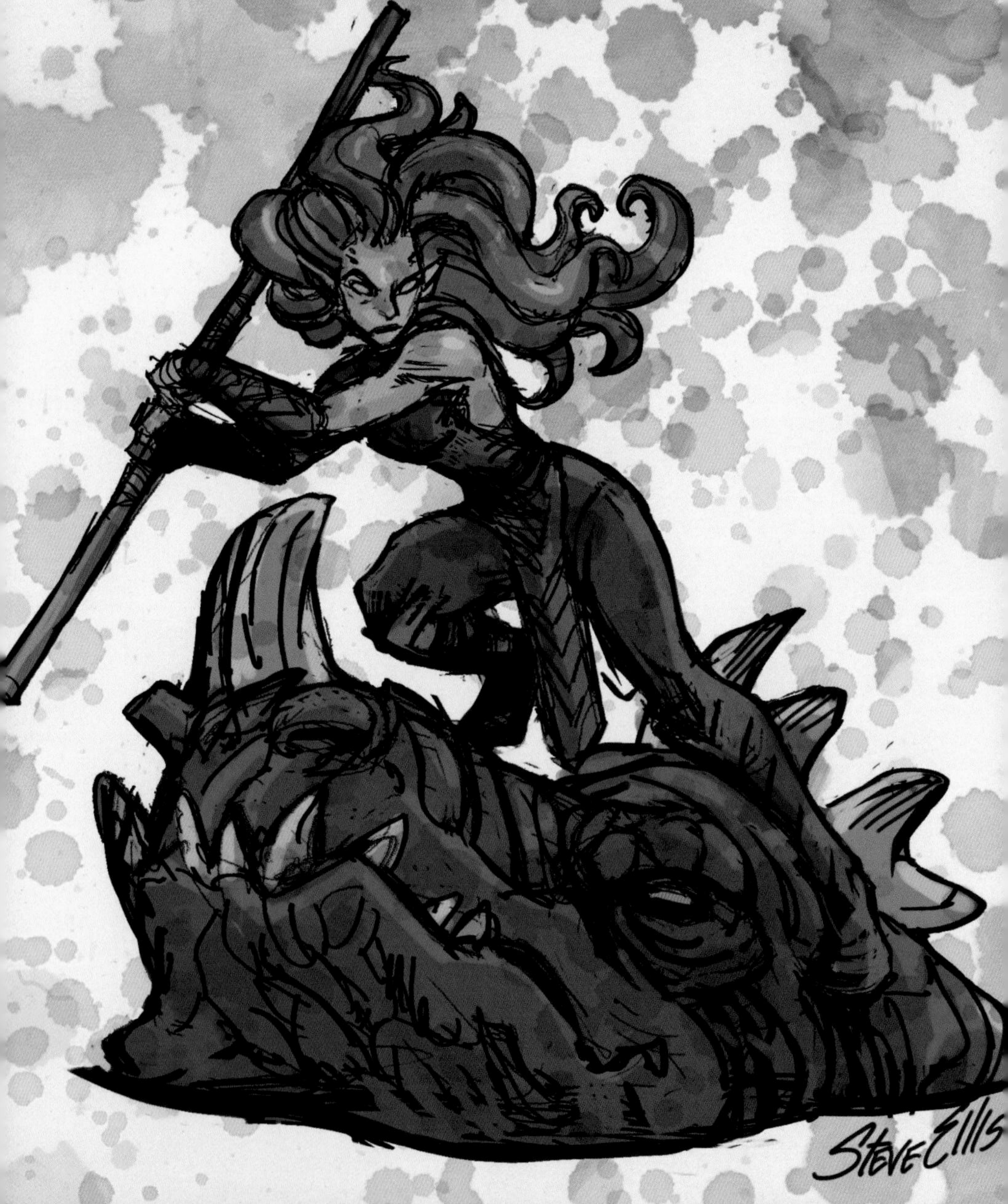
Steve Ellis

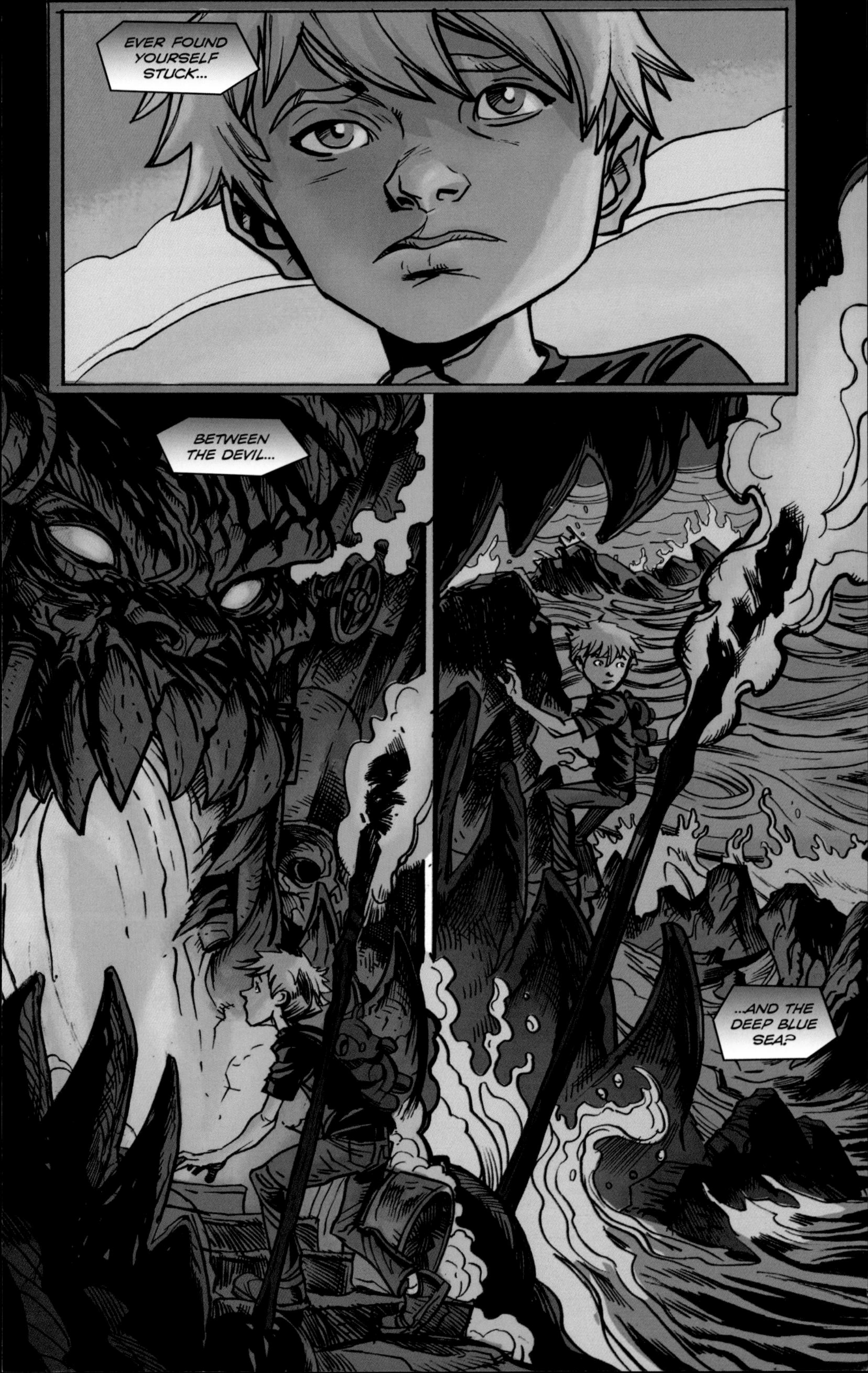
EVER FOUND YOURSELF STUCK...
BETWEEN THE DEVIL...
...AND THE DEEP BLUE SEA?

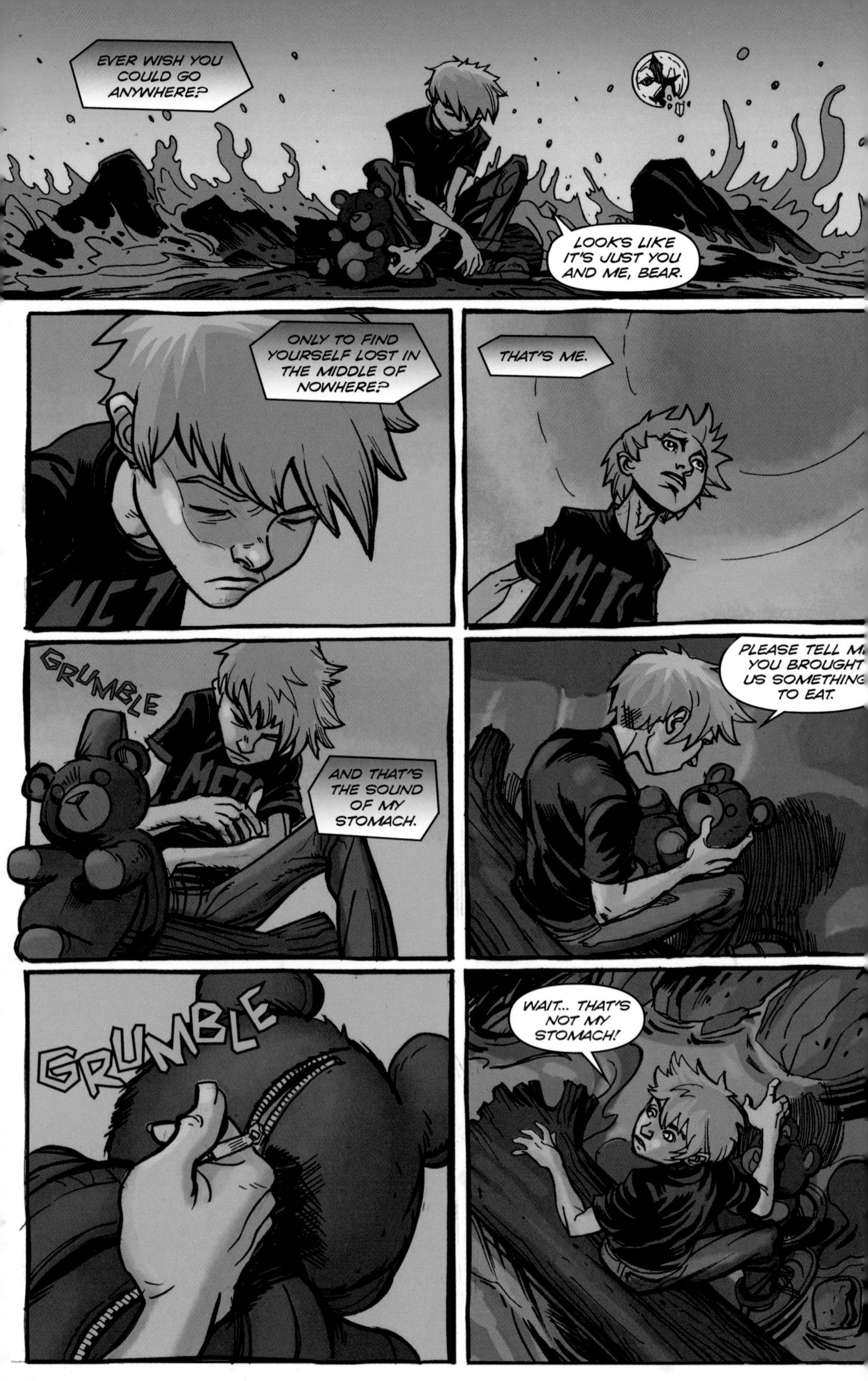

EVER WISH YOU COULD GO ANYWHERE?
LOOKS LIKE IT'S JUST YOU AND ME, BEAR.
ONLY TO FIND YOURSELF LOST IN THE MIDDLE OF NOWHERE?
THAT'S ME.
GRUMBLE
AND THAT'S THE SOUND OF MY STOMACH.
PLEASE TELL M YOU BROUGHT US SOMETHING TO EAT.
GRUMBLE
WAIT... THAT'S NOT MY STOMACH!

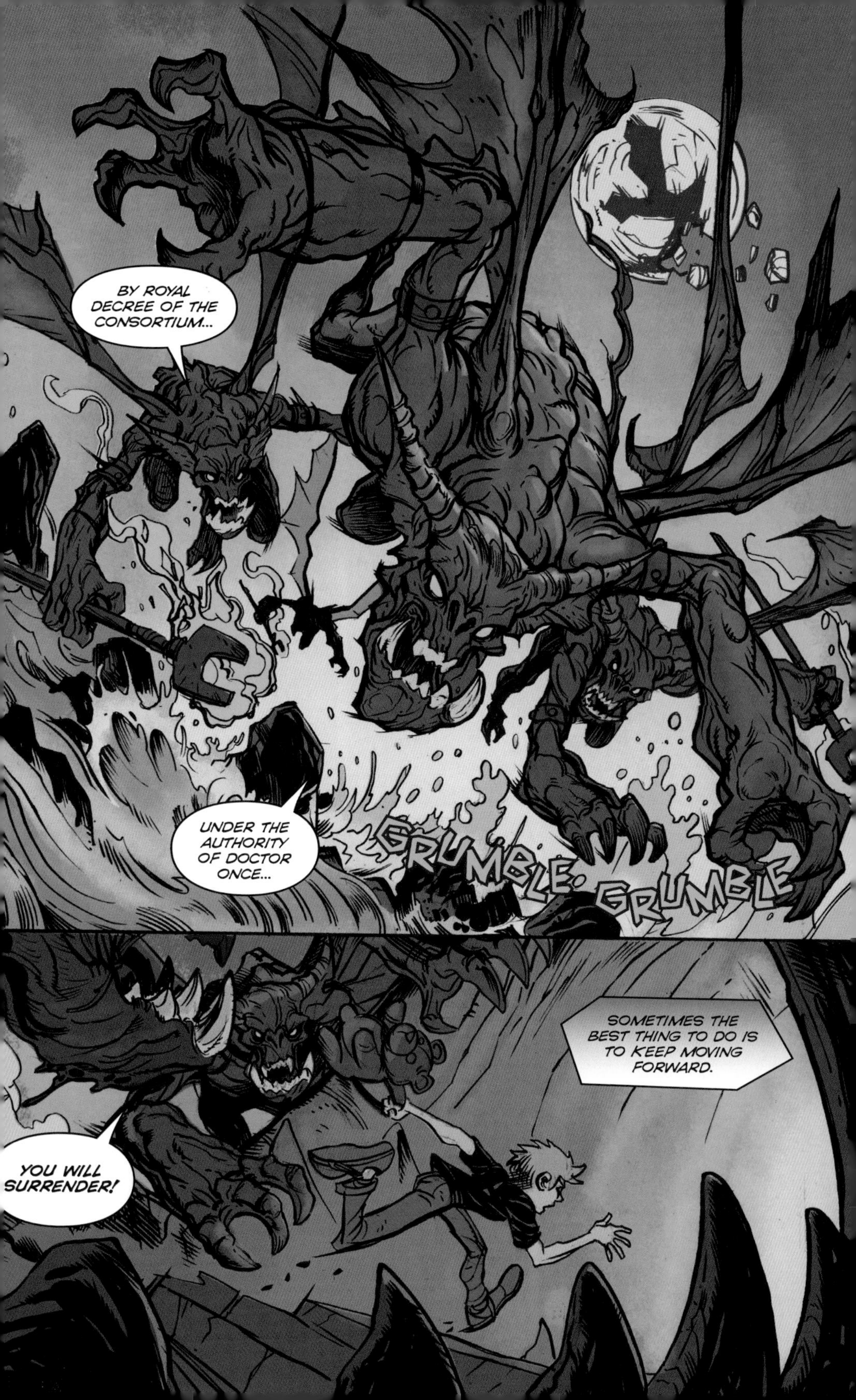
BY ROYAL DECREE OF THE CONSORTIUM...
UNDER THE AUTHORITY OF DOCTOR ONCE...
GRUMBLE GRUMBLE
SOMETIMES THE BEST THING TO DO IS TO KEEP MOVING FORWARD.
YOU WILL SURRENDER!

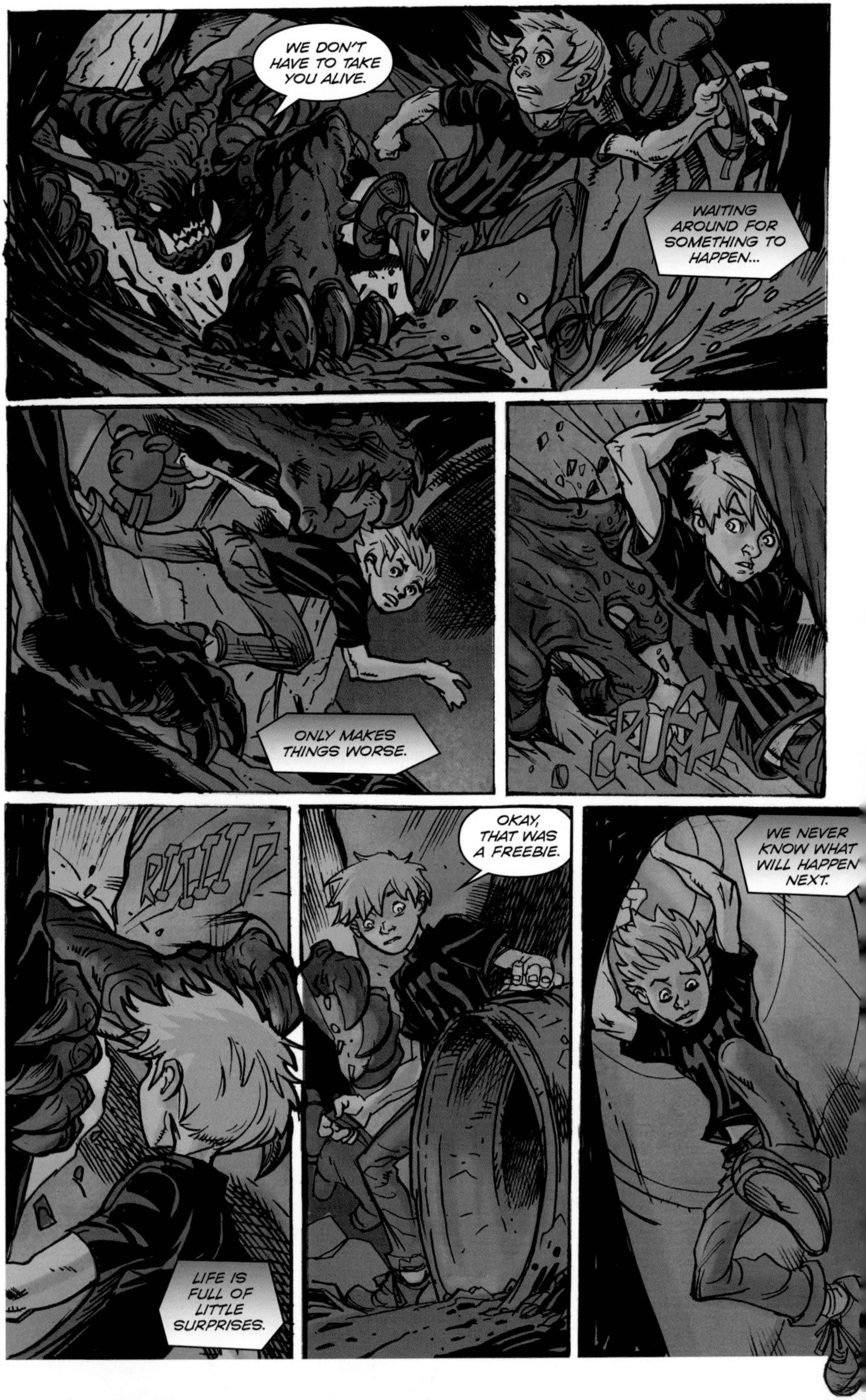
WE DON'T HAVE TO TAKE YOU ALIVE.
WAITING AROUND FOR SOMETHING TO HAPPEN...
ONLY MAKES THINGS WORSE.
CRUNCH
RIIIIP
LIFE IS FULL OF LITTLE SURPRISES.
OKAY, THAT WAS A FREEBIE.
WE NEVER KNOW WHAT WILL HAPPEN NEXT.

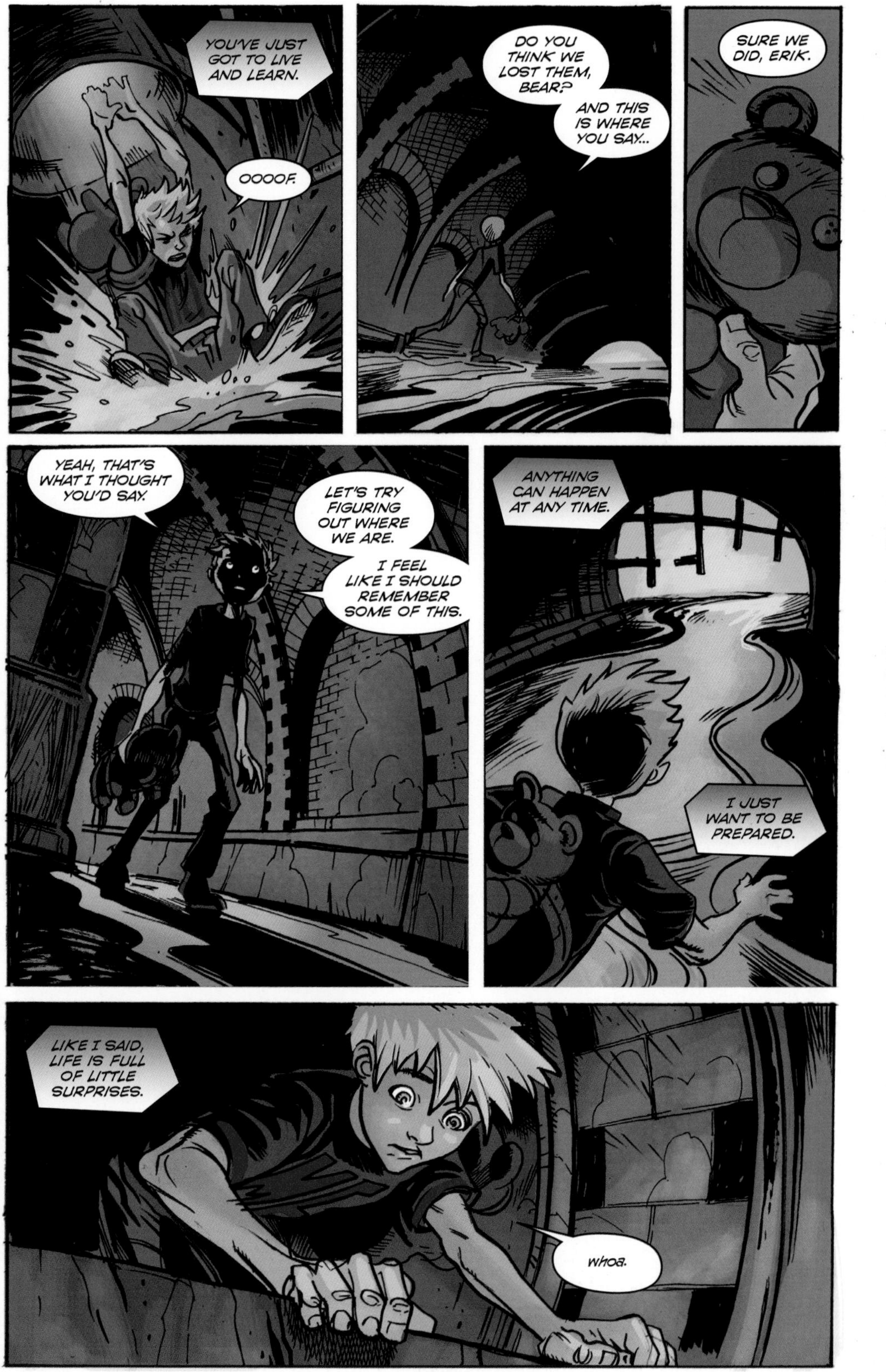
YOU'VE JUST GOT TO LIVE AND LEARN.
OOOOF.
DO YOU THINK WE LOST THEM, BEAR?
AND THIS IS WHERE YOU SAY...
SURE WE DID, ERIK.
YEAH, THAT'S WHAT I THOUGHT YOU'D SAY.
LET'S TRY FIGURING OUT WHERE WE ARE.
I FEEL LIKE I SHOULD REMEMBER SOME OF THIS.
ANYTHING CAN HAPPEN AT ANY TIME.
I JUST WANT TO BE PREPARED.
LIKE I SAID, LIFE IS FULL OF LITTLE SURPRISES.
whoa.

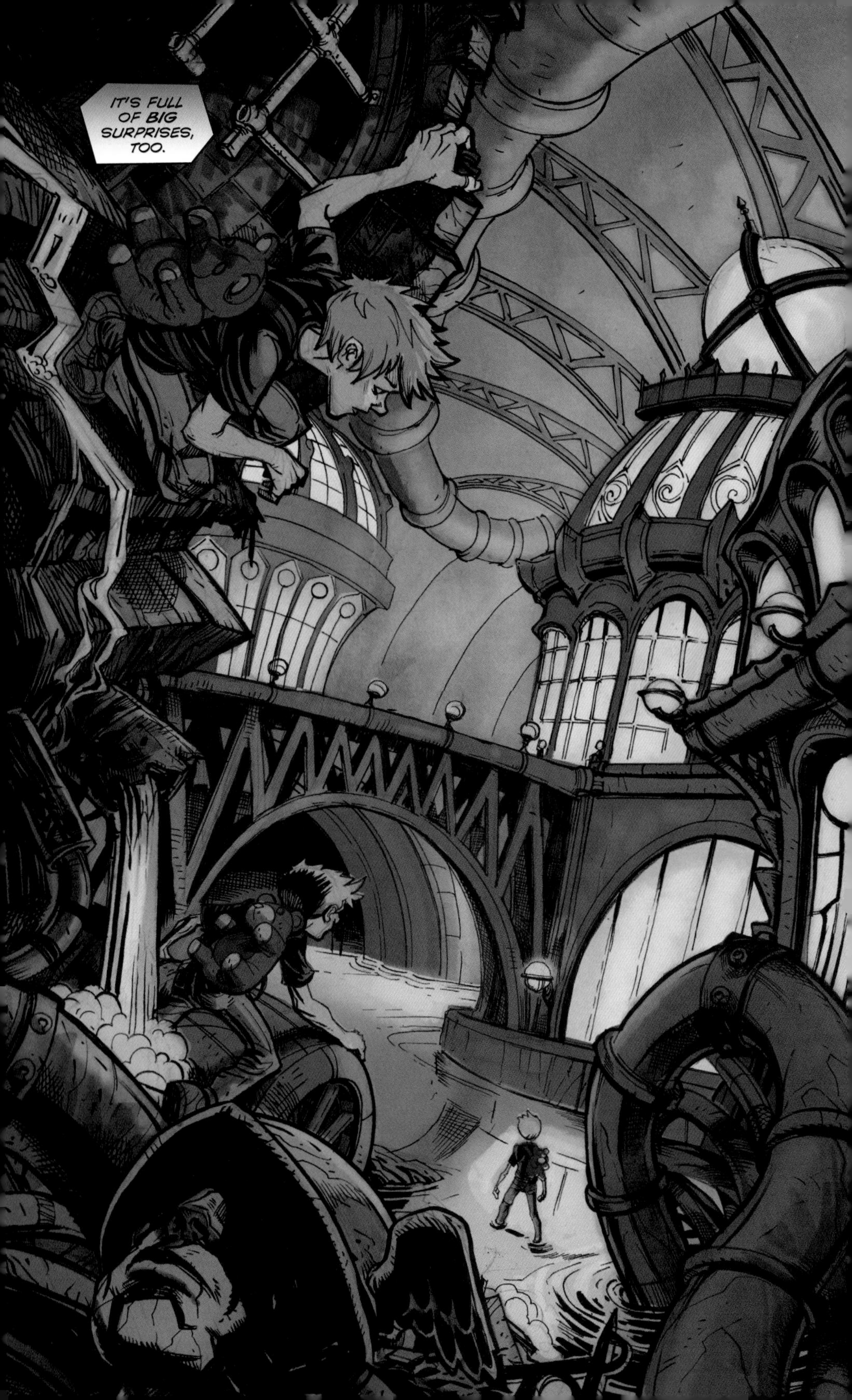
IT'S FULL OF BIG SURPRISES, TOO.

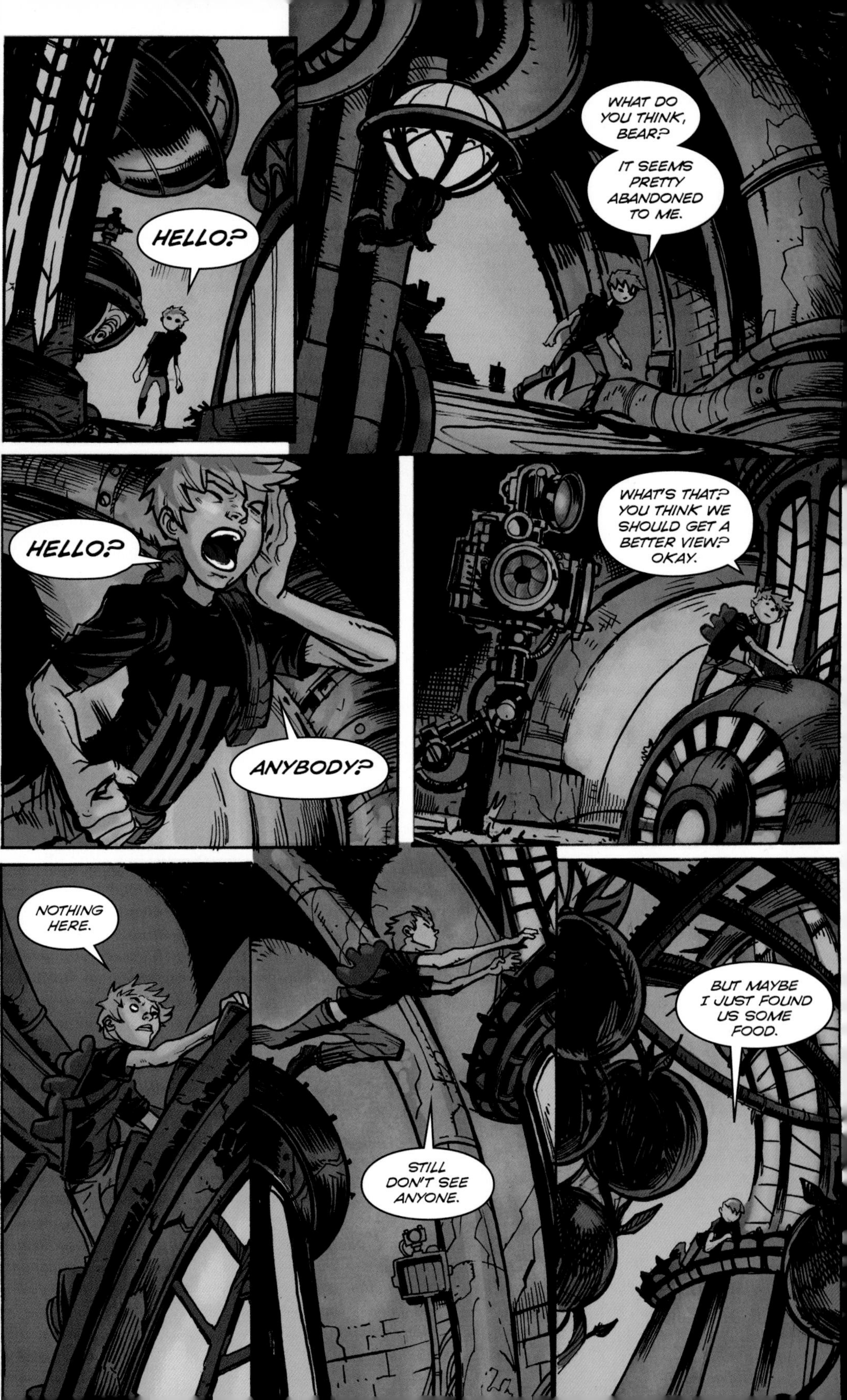
HELLO?
WHAT DO YOU THINK, BEAR?
IT SEEMS PRETTY ABANDONED TO ME.
HELLO?
ANYBODY?
WHAT'S THAT? YOU THINK WE SHOULD GET A BETTER VIEW? OKAY.
NOTHING HERE.
STILL DON'T SEE ANYONE.
BUT MAYBE I JUST FOUND US SOME FOOD.

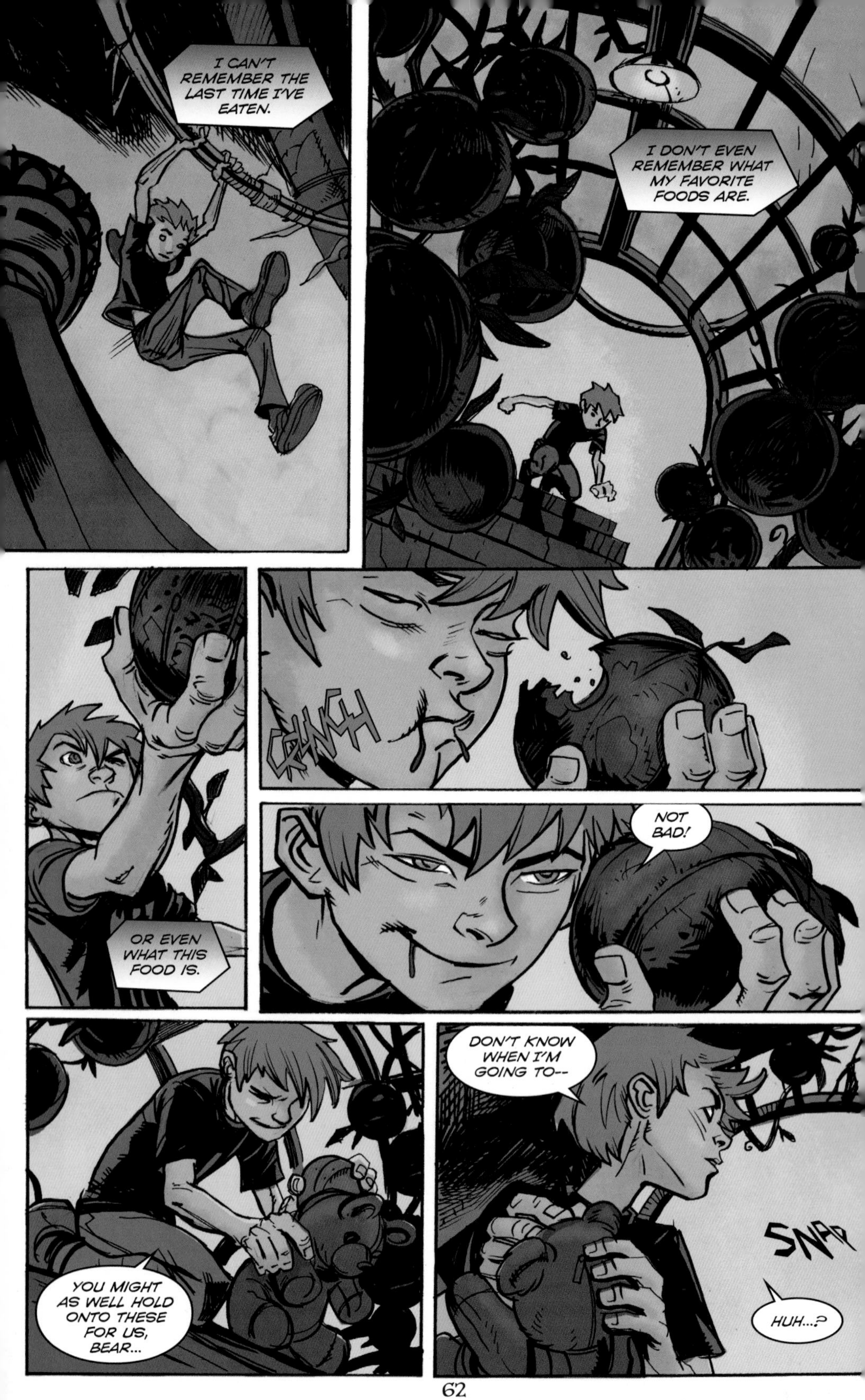
I CAN'T REMEMBER THE LAST TIME I'VE EATEN.
I DON'T EVEN REMEMBER WHAT MY FAVORITE FOODS ARE.
OR EVEN WHAT THIS FOOD IS.
CRUNCH
NOT BAD!
YOU MIGHT AS WELL HOLD ONTO THESE FOR US, BEAR...
DON'T KNOW WHEN I'M GOING TO--
SNAP
HUH...?

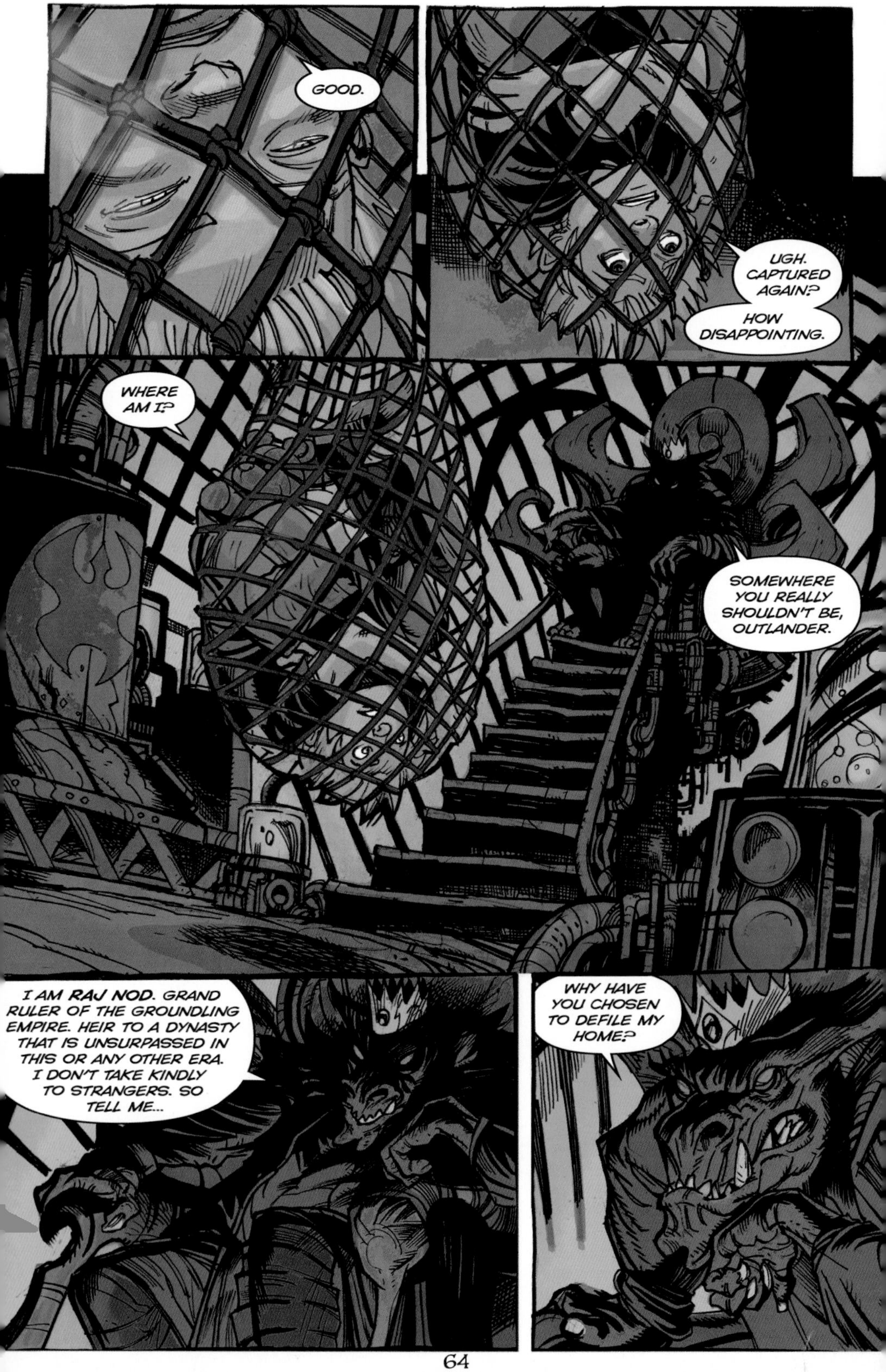
GOOD.
UGH. CAPTURED AGAIN?
HOW DISAPPOINTING.
WHERE AM I?
SOMEWHERE YOU REALLY SHOULDN'T BE, OUTLANDER.
I AM RAJ NOD. GRAND RULER OF THE GROUNDLING EMPIRE. HEIR TO A DYNASTY THAT IS UNSURPASSED IN THIS OR ANY OTHER ERA. I DON'T TAKE KINDLY TO STRANGERS. SO TELL ME...
WHY HAVE YOU CHOSEN TO DEFILE MY HOME?

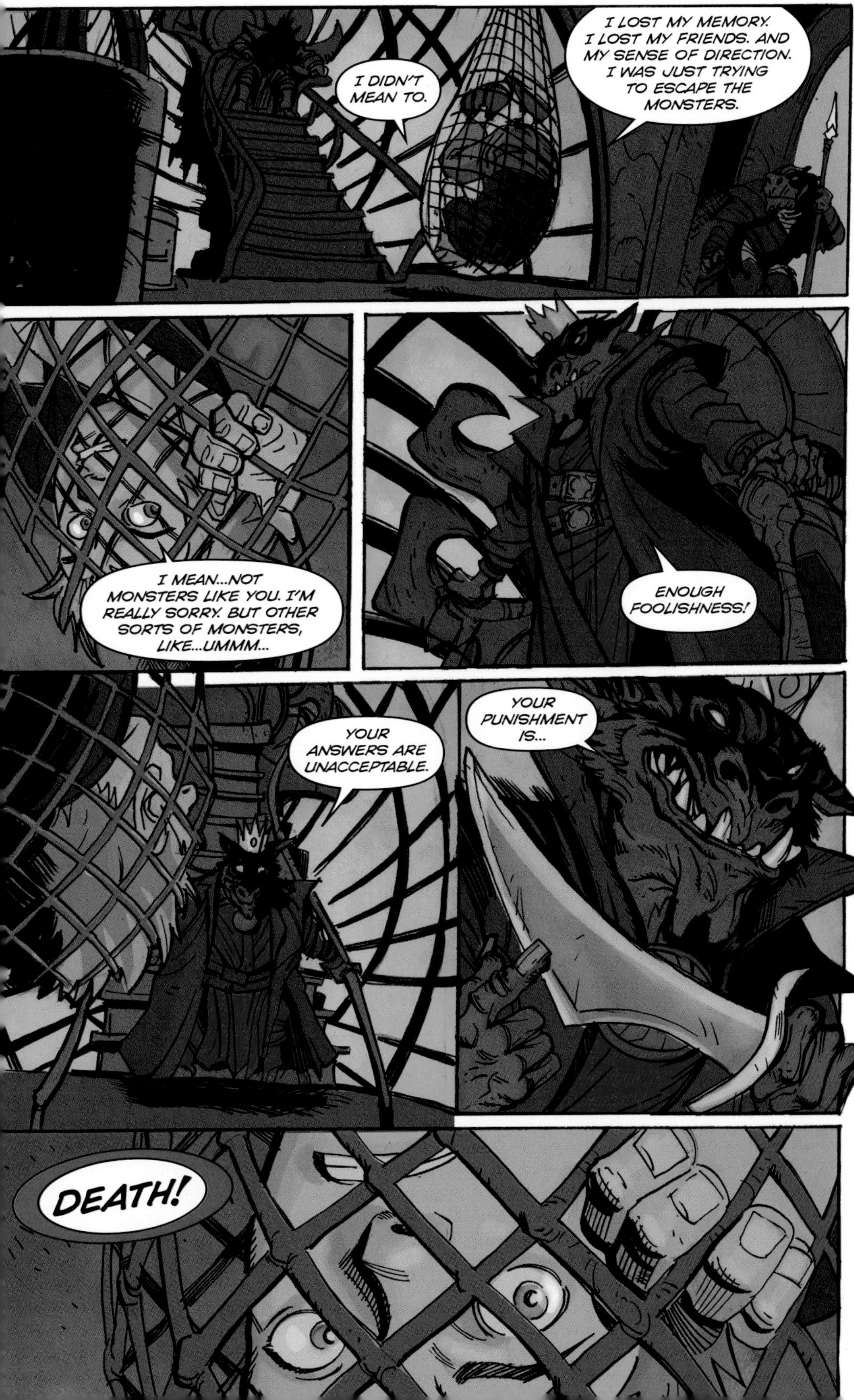
I DIDN'T MEAN TO.
I LOST MY MEMORY. I LOST MY FRIENDS. AND MY SENSE OF DIRECTION. I WAS JUST TRYING TO ESCAPE THE MONSTERS.
I MEAN...NOT MONSTERS LIKE YOU. I'M REALLY SORRY. BUT OTHER SORTS OF MONSTERS, LIKE...UMMM...
ENOUGH FOOLISHNESS!
YOUR ANSWERS ARE UNACCEPTABLE.
YOUR PUNISHMENT IS...
DEATH!

67

68

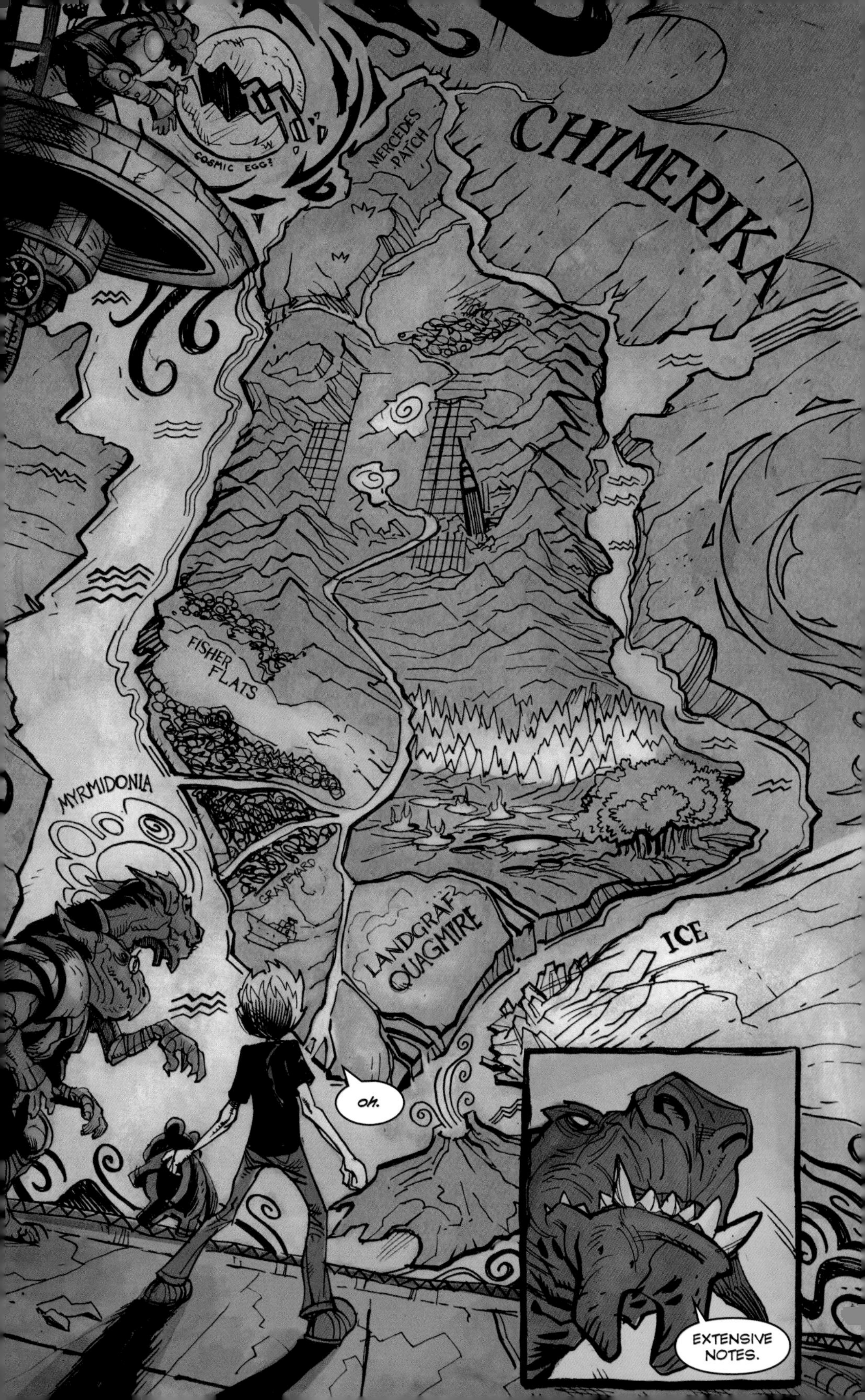

COSMIC EGG?
MERCEDES PATCH
CHIMERIKA
FISHER FLATS
MYRMIDONIA
GRAVEYARD
LANDGRAF QUAGMIRE
ICE
oh.
EXTENSIVE NOTES.

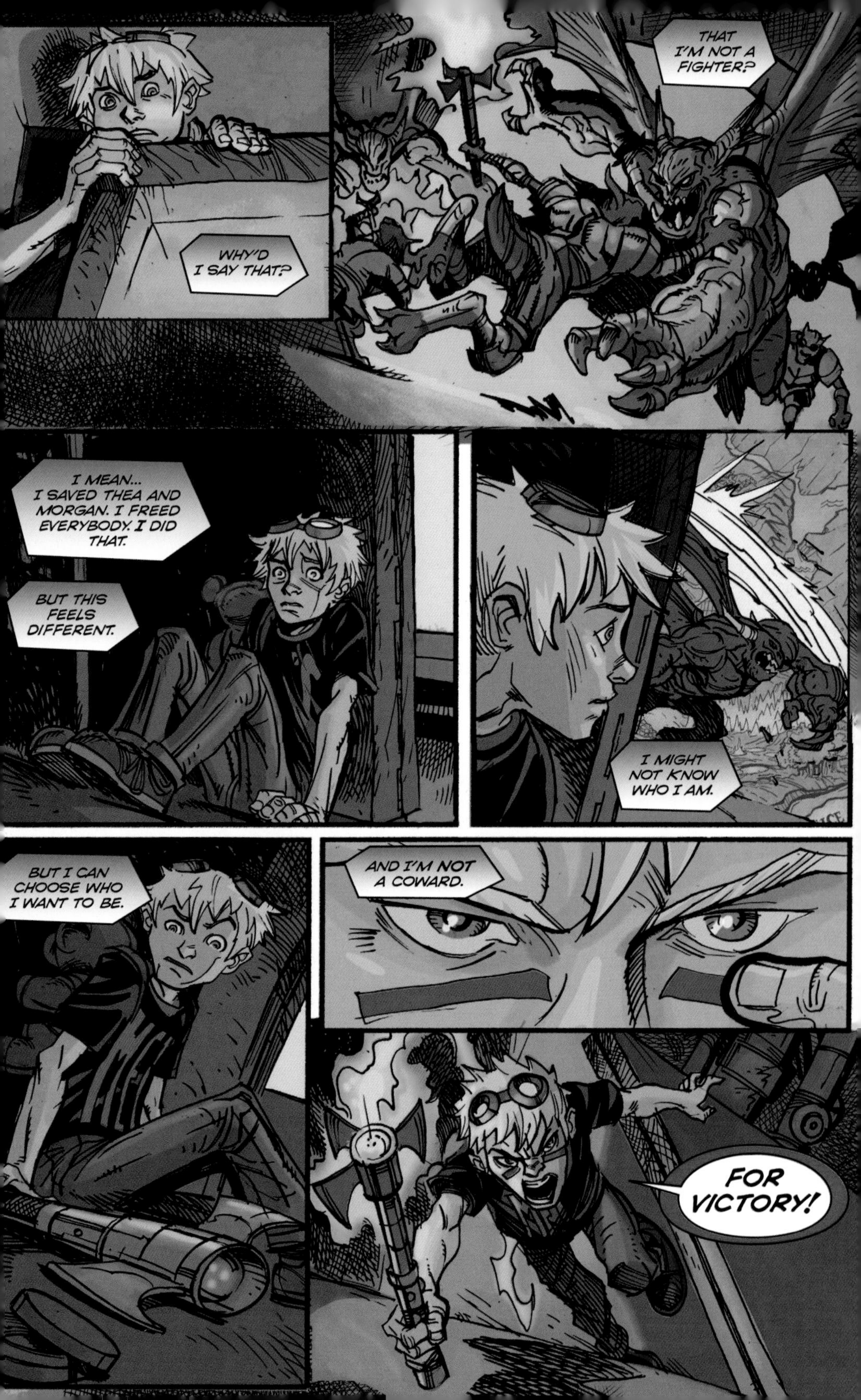
WHY'D
I SAY THAT?
THAT
I'M NOT A
FIGHTER?
I MEAN...
I SAVED THEA AND
MORGAN. I FREED
EVERYBODY. I DID
THAT.
BUT THIS
FEELS
DIFFERENT.
I MIGHT
NOT KNOW
WHO I AM.
BUT I CAN
CHOOSE WHO
I WANT TO BE.
AND I'M NOT
A COWARD.
FOR
VICTORY!

WATCH OUT FOR PAPERCUTZ™

Welcome to the pulse-pounding, perplexing-problems-packed, premiere THE ONLY LIVING BOY graphic novel, by David Gallaher and Steve Ellis from Papercutz–those seemingly still alive comic-makers dedicated to publishing graphic novels for all ages. I'm Jim Salicrup, the only sleeping Editor-in-Chief, and I'm here to take you behind the scenes–both at Papercutz and the world of THE ONLY LIVING BOY.

Let's start at the beginning. A little over ten years ago, Papercutz publisher Terry Nantier and I founded this little comicbook company to address a need–there just didn't seem to be enough comics and graphic novels for kids. That was incredibly ironic, since most folks think of comics as being for kids. After ten years of producing all types of comics for all ages, we made a great deal with the Dara Hyde at the Hill Nadell Agency, the agent for David and Steve, to publish the print version of their popular online comics series THE ONLY LIVING BOY. This particular webcomic has already garnered three Harvey Award nominations, including Best Original Graphic Publication for Younger Readers, but it was our erstwhile Production Coordinator Beth Scorzato who originally suggested that Papercutz should look into publishing it as a printed graphic novel series. Though limited-edition print editions have previously been sold by the creators at comic cons, Papercutz will proudly be offering our version–with all-new covers by Steve Ellis–through booksellers and comicbook stores, as well as through libraries.

For those of you not familiar with web comics, it's been quite the innovation. Theoretically, the Internet provides any would-be comics-creator worldwide distribution. Back in the Old Days, if comicbook writers and artists wished to self-publish their material, it was taking quite a risk, especially if they printed up comics before getting actual orders. With comics online, creators can post pages one at a time on a daily or weekly basis, with their only financial risk being their investment of time creating the comics. Eventually, enough pages are accumulated that collections, such as ours, are possible.

Many people wonder why a print edition is even necessary, and that's an excellent question. After all, why buy something (such as a book) when you can get the same material online for free? Makes sense, right? Yet one of the best-selling graphic novels series ever is *Diary of a Wimpy Kid* by Jeff Kinney (not to be confused with *Diary of Stinky Dead Kid*, which appeared in TALES FROM THE CRYPT #8 and #9, from Papercutz!), which started as a web comic–so go figure!

Unlike most Papercutz graphic novels which usually include self-contained stories, THE ONLY LIVING BOY is an ongoing series that's more in the tradition of ongoing comicbook series or ongoing TV series that tell stories that stretch out over several episodes. On the following pages, we're giving you a sneak peek at the second THE ONLY LIVING BOY graphic novel. We hope you enjoy it and return to find out what happens to Erik Farrell next in "Beyond Sea and Sky"!   Thanks,

Jim

Cover of the second limited-edtion THE ONLY LIVING BOY available only at comic conventions from David Gallaher and Steve Ellis.

STAY IN TOUCH!

EMAIL: salicrup@papercutz.com
WEB: papercutz.com
TWITTER: @papercutzgn
FACEBOOK: PAPERCUTZGRAPHICNOVELS
FAN MAIL: Papercutz, 160 Broadway, Suite 700,
              East Wing, New York, NY 10038

DAVID GALLAHER | STEVE ELLIS
THE ONLY LIVING BOY
#2
BEYOND SEA AND SKY
PAPERCUTZ

BEYOND SEA AND SKY

“Paul Pope and Jack Kirby never had a chance to work together, but if they had, it would be only slightly less awesome than this.”

—Mark Waid, writer, *Captain America, Daredevil, The Flash*

“David Gallaher and Steve Ellis have created a fantastic world in the literal and literary sense, and populated it with a menagerie of unforgettable characters. I loved taking this hero's journey with Erik, and so will you.”

—Ron Marz, writer, *Green Lantern, Silver Surfer*

COMING SOON!

THE ONLY LIVING BOY graphic novels are available for $8.99 in paperback, and $12.99 in hardcover. Available from booksellers everywhere. You can also order online from www.papercutz.com. Or call 1-800-886-1223, Monday through Friday, 9–5 EST. MC, Visa, and AmEx accepted. To order by mail, please add $4.00 for postage and handling for first book ordered, $1.00 for each additional book and make check payable to NBM Publishing. Send to: Papercutz, 160 Broadway, Suite 700, East Wing, New York, NY 10038.

PAPERCUTZ

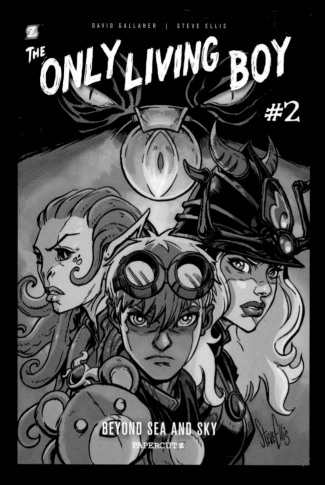

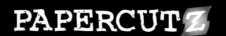

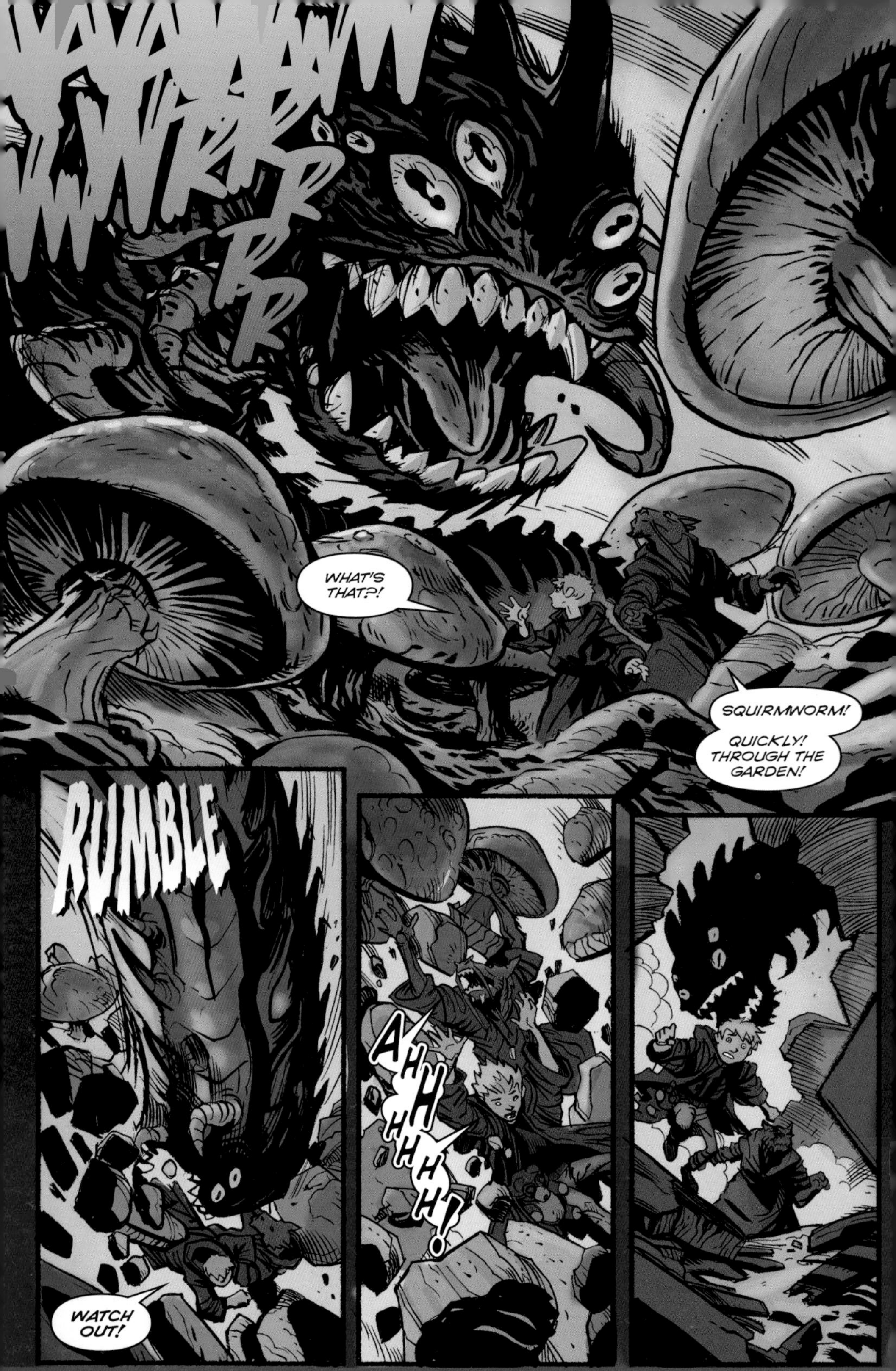

WHAT'S THAT?!
SQUIRMWORM!
QUICKLY! THROUGH THE GARDEN!
RUMBLE
WATCH OUT!
AHHHHHHH!

Don't Miss THE ONLY LIVING BOY #2 "Beyond Sea and Sky" Coming Soon.